Midnight Ferry
to Venice

Midnight Ferry to Venice

Ben Healy

WALKER AND COMPANY
New York

All the characters and events portrayed in this story are fictitious.

First published in the United States of America in 1982 by the Walker Publishing Company, Inc.

Published simultaneously in Canada by John Wiley & Sons Canada, Limited, Rexdale, Ontario.

ISBN: 0-8027-5461-9

Library of Congress Catalog Card Number: 81-70741

Printed in the United States of America

10 9 8 7 6 5 4 3 2 1

ONE

It started outside the Albergo Quattro Fontane on the Lungomare Marconi; a wide straight road with the sea, the bathing-beach of the Lido, rows of cabins and shrubbery on one side, and gardens and hotels on the other. A nice hotel, not so gilded as most of them here; the four well-heads and tables under the trees, and people sitting there in the shade taking their midday drinks. I had arrived in Venice two days before I was expected, travelling the slow and civilised way, still walking around and looking at things before starting work, and at this point thinking of a drink myself. And at this point also the girl came flying down the path between the flower-beds, and straight into my arms.

"Pardon me," she said, and I paused to look at her as I more or less set her on her feet again. "American," I thought; but one of the quiet sort. Small, and dark bronze hair with a glint of red in it, greenish blue eyes and a light powdering of freckles on the bridge of her nose; and, except that I have never seen a cat with freckles and a pair of enormous horn-rimmed spectacles, a sort of Burmese cat face. "Men seldom make passes at girls who wear glasses," I thought, and I like cats; but, before I could decide whether Miss Parker had been totally mistaken in that famous remark, the girl followed up with a question of such astonishing and abiding screwiness that it took my breath away. "Did you see the balloon seller?"

She made an impatient little gesture with her hands and arms and expression, sketching out something, and God knows how she did it—I was to discover later that this was a trick of hers, somehow creating an extraordinarily vivid image of something she had in her mind—but I had a fleeting picture of an old man in a long, dusty overall coat, a battered hat, and carrying a bunch of balloons floating above his head. She seemed to think that I had disappeared him, looking at me rather severely. "He was here a minute ago."

I looked up and down the Lungomare myself. Opulent motor-cars, the little beach-buggy things the gilded hotels provide for their inmates in case walking too much should wear them out, a film-camera van, all sorts and colours of clothes and humanity, a bunch of starlets flashing dentifrice smiles from the entrance to the Exelsior, and an elderly carrozza ambling towards us; but no balloons. I shook my head. "Perhaps he took off? I mean, it's a hot day, and if he had a lot of balloons and he was a very small man . . . .? Did you want a balloon then?"

She glanced up into the sky involuntarily, but the impression I got this time was that I was something worse than fatuous. "I do *not* want a balloon. I want that balloon man."

"Yes," I said. "I quite understand. But that's different, isn't it?" And this is interesting, I thought.

This is worth following up. Delusions come in all shapes and sizes, but delusions about balloon men must be almost unique. Even for the Lido that had a sort of harlequinade improbability about it. "Well," I said, "the best place to find balloon men is obviously the Viale Elizabetta. You can find almost anything there. And the best way is from a carrozza. You can see the balloons floating above the crowds."

She gave me a glance like a cat which is more hurt than offended. "I'm sorry to have bothered you. Please think no more of it."

"But you have bothered me," I told her, putting up my hand to stop the carrozza. "And it's a thing I shall think of for hours; days probably. I shall be haunted by a balloon man."

Her eyes were flashing sparks of green fire behind the horn rims. "Not you. *Me. I'm* haunted by one."

"It's a distressing condition." And quite a nasty little temper with it, I thought, as the carrozza creaked up alongside us. The horse was wearing a straw hat with a blue ribbon, and that was beautiful too; the final surrealist touch. What surprises me now is that I did not then realise that surrealism can be sinister as well. I opened the carriage door instead, saying, "Jump in. You haven't lived if you've never driven down the Gran Viale Santa Maria Elizabetta in a carrozza. It's the next best thing to being royalty. We'll hunt your balloon seller together. If he was here a minute ago and he's not here now he's probably lurking in one of the gardens; busily puncturing all his balloons one by one so you can't spot him."

"It would be very, very impolite as we don't know each other," she said. "But in just one more minute I shall take a swipe at you."

All the same she climbed up into the carriage and we started to clop along the Lungomare, the horse half asleep on its feet. I told the man to take us to Marco's

Bar, and he nodded just as sleepily; and I went on, "Talking of not knowing each other. Hedley. Paul Hedley; of London, England."

"I am very pleased to make your acquaintance." Though she did not sound particularly pleased; and solemn with it. "Judith Elaine Harford; Boston. It's a very old name. My great-great-grandfather came from your Hampshire."

"Then we're practically cousins. Somebody once said that if you go back far enough everybody is related."

She did not seem to be particularly pleased about that either, and there was a short silence. She was watching the gardens on our left as we crawled past them, and there was no doubt that she was worried. Not surprisingly perhaps. If I kept having delusions about balloon sellers I should get worried; though as a class they appear to be fairly harmless, and I could imagine worse fantasies to have. This need not prove fatal, I thought. Thereby demonstrating once again my inborn genius for famous last words on several counts. But the silence was getting rather protracted, and I murmured, "Speaking of balloon men," and nodded towards the beach and the bathing-cabins, "there's one."

She turned as quickly as a startled cat, but then only gave this man a single quick glance. Disappointed, or relieved? It was impossible to tell which. "The wrong shape," she said. They were of the sausage variety, and she was short about it. "Those my man was carrying were all round ones."

We were turning into the Viale then, with our driver now visibly asleep. A kaleidoscope: trees, flower-boxes, cannas, geraniums, awnings, parasols, and a slowly drifting crowd between the tables. It seemed to take her mind off balloons for a minute.

"It's very, very pretty. Do you think we should wake the driver?"

"Not necessarily, so long as the horse stays half awake. He's seen it all before."

She considered that remark more carefully than it deserved before saying the next thing. "I would not like to have you thinking that I make a habit of riding around with persons I don't know."

"Of course not. But I've just said, we're practically cousins. And hunting balloon men tends to throw people together."

Another little green flash, a little cat with claws if she chose to use them; and another silence, which gave me a chance to look at her more closely. A neat figure, nicely turned in the right places, but nothing too ostentatious; a sleeveless, pale-green linen dress, good but not too expensive; a tiny mole high up on her right cheek. Rather prim and decidedly self-contained; but certainly with something on her mind. She turned and caught me looking at her, flushing. "And what brings you to Venice, Mr. Hedley? Are you on vacation?"

"Not exactly." I was watching a film-camera car cruising slowly up alongside us, a Land-Rover type of vehicle with a platform mounted on the roof; the camera panning on the crowds. "I'm here to paint a portrait."

There was a spark of interest this time. "You're an artist; a painter?"

"I think so. Some people agree with me. Others don't."

That camera car had been outside the Exelsior with the starlets a few minutes ago, but of course there was nothing to it. To anybody making a film in Venice a shot of the crowds strolling on the Viale Elizabetta is obligatory. The camera was holding a pretty small girl staggering along with an inflatable beach-toy as big as herself, but then as it drew abreast and ahead it swung round on to the carrozza; the cameraman bearded, long haired, leather jacket and jeans, all slightly scruffy. All quite typical, and nothing in that either; a pretty girl in a carrozza with the driver and horse both more than half asleep is all part of the scene too. But he was holding us in focus for a long time; several feet of film at least.

And then Miss Harford chose to go into action. She said, "Hey!" and leaned forward to prod our driver in the back; I had a vision of a Victorian lady prodding a cabby with the point of her umbrella. The driver woke with a start and several remarks which made me hope Miss Harford did not understand Italian, his horse very nearly fell down with surprise, then turned its head to cast a reproachful look from under the straw hat, and set off at a positively reckless amble; while I protested, You don't want to go doing things like that, it upsets the horse; he's not built for chariot racing," and Miss Harford called, "*Presto! Presto!*" and added triumphantly, "There!"

By this time I had lost sight of the camera car, and of course it was balloons again; as round as anybody could wish for, floating above the heads of the crowd, and Miss Harford saying, "Stop; *arreste*; hold it!" pointing across the pavement and calling, "Hey! You there."

For such a small girl she had a surprising volume, and it seemed to be her balloon seller all right. Long, dusty brown coat like an engineer's overall, tattered straw hat and drooping moustache, a face like a more than disillusioned old monkey. He looked worried too, and for a second I thought he was going to bolt, but the crowd and several small dogs were now scenting interest and it was difficult for him to get through. He asked instead, "You wanna buy a balloon?"

He sounded somewhat incredulous about it, and she

announced, "I do *not* want to buy a balloon. I want a word with *you*, my man. I want to know why you are *haunting* me these last two days."

He shook his head; and he had an American accent far more noticeable than hers. "Lady, I never seen you in my life before."

"You lie,"she announced, as if she were announcing the American Declaration of Independence, and started counting on her fingers. "The day before yesterday, four-twenty p.m. at the railroad terminus. And there was also a man seling disgusting little yellow dogs which made horrid squeaking noises in a bucket of water; and an ice-cream vendor, and a newspaper vendor, and a man with silk . . ."

"No," I cut in. "Not everybody outside the station. It'll get out of hand. Let's keep it to balloon sellers, Judy. They're quite enough to be going on with."

"Miss Harford," she snapped between her teeth, and went on counting. "The day before yesterday, five-ten p.m. at the San Marco ferry station. That same evening, eight p.m. outside the Grand Hotel, here. Yesterday morning, ten a.m. at the Accademia del' Arti. Twelve noon at the Biblioteca Querini. Eight p.m., last night at the Grand Hotel again. Eleven forty-five this morning at the Quattro Fontane." She paused for a breath, and somebody raised a cheer. "And I mean to know why," she finished.

"*Mama mia,*" the balloon man started. But the crowd was thickening, and he was not quite sure where the sympathy lay. "You don't wanna buy a balloon, so why're you picking on me?" he screamed. "I told you, lady, I never seen you in my life before. Say," he asked me confidentially, "is she nuts?"

"A touch of the sun, the poor soul," one of the women murmured. "It strikes very suddenly."

"That's true," our driver agreed, nodding heavily. "She doesn't have a hat," he added, no doubt thinking of his horse. "You should get a hat," he advised me severely. "I have a friend who sells most beautiful hats."

It was very nearly fatal. I saw Miss Harford gathering herself for something; in another minute everybody would have joined in, and across the road there were two carabinieri watching the scene with interest. I pushed a thousand-lire note at the balloon seller—always the cowardly way, but always the safest—muttering, "Beat it," and said, "Wake lightning up, and let's go. It's all a big misunderstanding," I explained to the crowd.

We lurched off again with the horse doing a double shuffle this time, cocking its blue ribbon even more rakishly over one eye. I said nothing; the driver said something hopefully about hats; Miss Harford said nothing. She was pink under the nice soft brown, simmering quietly, and there were still green sparkles in her eyes. But there was also an air of quiet triumph about her, and it took me a minute or two to realise that she was trying to prevent herself laughing; and, oddly enough, that was where I started to get worried.

Nothing was said until we got to Marco's and the horse and driver staggered away, both half asleep again before they were out of sight. Then when Marco found us a place on the sidewalk, from which I could see both sides of the road, she announced, "I should tell you that I don't drink," but added honestly, "not at this time of the day."

"Some time, perhaps," I said, rather irritably. "I do; constantly. Now about this balloon seller . . ."

"You are not an addict, I hope?" she enquired. "Painters sometimes lead very dissolute lives."

"Mine is in the last stages of dissolution. But about your balloon man . . ."

"I consider the matter is now settled." She awarded Marco a kindly smile. "An *aranciata,* if you please;

with ice. I was irritated, but I consider I have proved my point. And do I *look* as if I would wish to buy a balloon?"

"A Lowenbrau," I told Marco, and said feelingly, "You don't. But I hope it is settled."

"It is. That man will certainly not haunt me again." I thought that particular man might not, but the orange juice arrived then, and she gazed at me over the glass—a sort of eager interest. "Let's forget it. Tell me about the portrait you have to paint."

"There's not much to tell. It's a rather elderly lady. Apparently a rather fearsome old lady. A sort of Grand Dame of Venice. But that's as much as I know myself so far. I have to call the Ca' Silvestro this afternoon and say, 'Please, I'm here.' "

The interest was real and quick this time. "Did you say the Ca' Silvestro? How very odd. How very, very odd."

"What's so odd about it?" I asked.

She did not answer at first; but got suddenly just as interested in her orange juice, tinkling the ice-cubes about in it. "It's odd the way we met. Do tell me, Mr. Hedley, how was this arranged? I'm a very inquisitive person, I'm afraid."

"Through my agent."

She was obviously about to ask one more question, but changed her mind. "And who . . . Is that how these things are usually done?

"They can be done any number of ways. It just happened in this case."

She nodded. "You will pardon my asking? But I'm very interested. That's what my family always say. They say, 'Judith, you're interested in just *too* many things.' "

"I get touches of the same trouble. You, for instance. And balloon men. Are you here on holiday? And what do you do when you're not?"

"Well . . ." She seemed to be weighing exactly what

to say. "I like to make my work a vacation. I'm a historical student. At present with particular reference to Queen Christina of Sweden."

Slightly screwy again, I thought; getting surrealist once more. I said, "That sounds harmless enough. But shouldn't it be in Rome?"

"Perhaps." She seemed to be looking for a reaction, and slightly puzzled because she did not get one. Then she glanced at her watch, and the party was over. "My! So *late!* I must fly."

I said, "Wait a minute. If you start seeing balloon men again, or other people who irritate you, I'm at the Pensione Martinelli; on the Via Lepanto." It was a fair offer, and not entirely because I liked her nice little brown cat face; but she showed no sign of taking it up, and I tried another line. "Have lunch with me."

"I'd really like to." All the heartfelt regret in the world. "It's too bad; but I've another appointment. And I'm late already."

At the Grand Hotel? I wondered, watching her slip through the crowd. The Grand Hotel last night, and the night before; just in time for dinner. And why not?

When Marco came to pick up the empty glass I was at work on the back of one of his tariff cards with a soft pencil. I have the knack of a quick caricature portrait, and the balloon seller's drooping moustache and disillusioned monkey face under the balloons made him an easy one. The look in Marco's eye was obviously saying "No luck today then?" but I asked, "Do you know this character?"

"That's smart, eh?" he said. "Sure. Luigi Antonello. Bit of a bum. Most often works the Rialto, but comes over here now and again."

"Next time you see him you might tell him I'd like a word." I rubbed my thumb and forefinger together in the age-old gesture signifying money. "Tell him I'll always be here about this time of day, and in the evenings just before dinner. And would you know any of the staff at the Grand Hotel?" Marco made his own little gesture indicating that he might or he might not, and I nodded. "The same applies. Preferably one of the dining-room waiters or a bell boy."

I have always considered that bar-keepers are among the most useful classes in the civilised world.

I must go back a bit; about three weeks to my agent, Manny Levin, and in London. Manny is a good agent and a very good friend, and I would do anything for him; or anything within reason. When Manny is working on a prospective buyer he is all of Bond Street, Fifth Avenue and the Champs Elysées, but when he gets excited he slips into natural Bronx with a touch or two of points east of Warsaw. He was very excited that morning; and before he had got a dozen words out I guessed that even he thought there was something odd about this proposition. He started, "Say, Pol, you don't have nothing on you can't drop, do you? So have you seen the news today, and what d'ya know about the weather? So how'd you like a trip to Venice? Maybe a month or so?"

"I'd sooner not see the news," I said, "and I don't want to know about the weather. That makes the answer 'No' to the first and 'Yes' to the second. But what for?"

"I got a portrait commission for you. Very nice. Beautiful. Good money." He seemed to turn careful suddenly, slightly wheedling as if he was nervous I might turn it down. "A Mrs.. Amelita Messina-Silvestro; a real, top-line Venetian socialite. Listen, Pol; don't cut in yet. Let me tell you. She ain't what you're thinking. She's pushing sixty-five. I been checking on her. From what I hear she's kind of Queen of Venice. Palazzo, committees, charities, you name it, she's in it. A widow. You know what the word is of her husband's last breath when he died? He said, 'Lord, now lettest thou thy servant depart in peace.' Now why would a man say a thing like that?"

"I can guess. But why does she want me in particular?"

"Because you're good, boy. Pol, how often do I have to tell you it ain't just enough to be good? You have to get the right folks to tell the world you're good. That's what we been doing."

"And who's 'we'?"

Manny turned cautious again. "There's a guy named Harcourt d'Espinal. Sir Harcourt d'Espinal. Seems he recommended you. Do you know him?"

I cast my mind back. A few years ago, a sensation. Articles in the glossy art journals and the quality week-ends. A party I went to and a big man there shedding benevolence on all; my own impression that all he needed was a Roman toga and a gilded laurel wreath. "I met him once. A character like Robert Morley playing the part of one of the more amiable Roman emperors. Didn't he discover an uncatalogued Botticelli somewhere?"

"That's it, boy. You got him. So he makes a trade of tracing lost works of art now. There's plenty of 'em to find. And he's a top-line expert on the Quattrocento and Cinquecento. That's for sure." Manny paused fractionally. "There might be other things that ain't just so certain about him."

"Such as he's a crook?"

"Hold it now," Manny protested. "I never said that. Don't go putting words into your Uncle Manny's mouth. So maybe he's a crook. So what? So it ain't catching, is it? So you ain't narrow-minded? See now, Pol; like I told you, it's good money.

He mentioned a fee which surprised me. "What does the woman want?" I asked. "An ikon? Look, Manny, doesn't it strike you that there's a loud smell of fish about this?"

"Sure," he agreed. He paused again and then went on, "Do me a favour, will you? See now, Pol, I'll tell you. There's something going to break out there, and it's something big. I can't just guess what it is; but the grapevine's been buzzing, and I'd sure like to know. Seems there's two, three folks going to be in Venice. One of 'em's Dr. Hans Kleber of Munich. Maybe you've heard of him as well."

"Yes," I said. "I've heard of him. He's another expert. All right, Manny; I'll go. After all that I couldn't resist it, could I?"

"There's my boy. So I'll fix it right away." He was in a hurry suddenly. "You should be getting letters any time."

The odd atmosphere went on at Mrs. Messina-Silvestro's cocktail-party later that day, after I had met our Miss Harford for the first time. This party was a surprise item. I was expected on the twelfth of May, and in the several letters we had exchanged—two from Mrs. Messina-Silvestro's secretary, and one from d'Espinal recommending the Pensione Martinelli and advising me obliquely that the old lady liked a certain amount of formality; as if he was afraid that I might turn up in jeans and a check shirt—I had arranged to call the house in the afternoon. It was about three o'clock then, and the first voice I got was a male, sleepy, decidedly Cockney and more than slightly liquor-laden. It said, "'Allo?" and then corrected itself to "Pronto; the Ca' Silvestro", went on, "Ooh, you won't get '*er*" when I asked for Mrs. Messina, then did another correction. "Just one moment, sir."

The next one was a woman, and faintly American again; the secretary and companion. "Mr. Hedley? This is Celia van Druyten. Mrs. Messina-Silvestro is resting at the moment. We were wondering if you had arrived yet. So good of you to call so promptly. We've been looking forward to meeting you. And apropos of that, Mrs. Messina is giving a small party tonight; just a few people from six to eight. If it's not too short notice I wonder if we might ask you to join us? It would be very convenient, don't you think? To break the ice, as it were."

I agreed that it would be an excellent ice-breaker, and said that I would take the ferry across to San Marco and pick up a taxi there, but she cut in, "My dear Mr. Hedley, Mrs. Messina-Silvestro would be most distressed. I'll send our motor-boat for you. Our man will come to your hotel to meet you. It will save confusion." Confusion? I thought fleetingly; it's an odd word to use, but she went on, "There are always so many boats milling about Santa Elizabetta at that time of the evening. Shall we say six o'clock then?"

And prompt on six he was there, waiting at the reception with the proprietor, Signor Martinelli, saying quietly, "This is Mr. Hedley"; apparently natural enough, but it still looked as if they were making sure that I was who I claimed to be. He was polite but tough-looking, and nobody comes tougher than a tough Venetian; hard, watchful blue eyes and a well-cut sort of half nautical uniform; so well cut that I thought I could make out the bulge of a pistol under the jacket. But I could have been imagining that. After balloon sellers and Miss Harford today, an abbreviated conversation which never got round to explanations, and after Celia van Druyten on the telephone, I could have imagined almost anything.

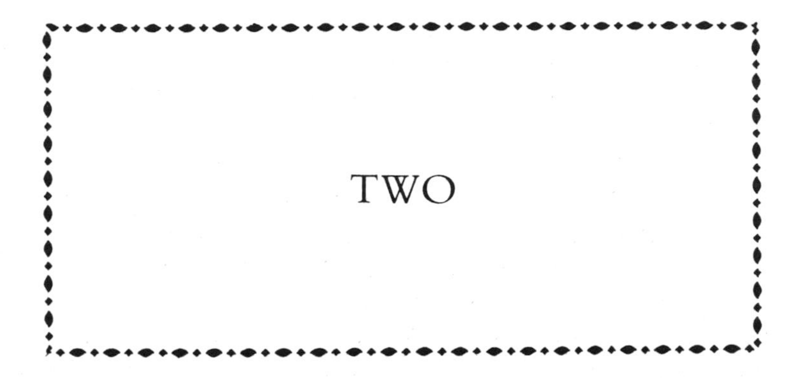

TWO

The Ca' Silvestro was just beyond the Rialto Bridge, on a quiet siding off the flashing spectacle of the Grand Canal; the oldest part of Venice, where the city was originally founded. Time eroded arches and quays, dark green water lapping softly at worn stone and crumbling dark red brick, and our boat cruising along so quietly that it scarcely raised a ripple. A secretive, gloomy spot at night, I thought; and the building itself could hardly be called a palazzo. By comparison with many on the Grand Canal it was neither very large, ornate, or particularly old; it looked like early eighteenth century superimposed on a more ancient foundation, and from the incongruous tubular steel scaffolding around some parts it was undergoing extensive restoration.

Could I have known it this rebuilding was an important factor in the whole story, but at that time I thought it was merely part of the general effort to try and save Venice from sinking, and I was more interested in the two carabinieri standing on the quay, bored but watchful; then once in the entrance hall, with one of the boatmen leading the way, the slight air of unreality took over again. There were signs of work going on here too; but like many Venetian houses, with the water quietly rising higher every year, this was little more than an enclosed courtyard and a flight of worn marble stairs leading up to the residential quarters above. There was a butler waiting at the foot of them, striped trousers and cut-away coat, a rosy face, thatch of white hair and shrewd little eyes; clearly the cockney voice which had answered the telephone the first time this afternoon. The boatman said, "Signor Hedley," and and the butler repeated solemnly, "Mr. 'Edley. If you will follow me, sir."

There was the faintest whiff of cloves in the atmosphere as he marched up the stairs as though carrying a bottle of old crusted port, and I murmured softly, "I hope I didn't disturb your sleep this afternoon."

"As a matter of fact you did," he muttered out of the side of his mouth. I barely saw his lips move. "We don't like telephone calls between two and 'alf-past four. Don't do it again if you can 'elp it."

"I won't," I promised. "I shall have to get to know the house-rules. You'll have to tell me. What's your name?"

"Carson, sir." A hoarse whisper floating back. "And always willing to oblige."

It was a wide, carpeted corridor now, antique Florentine furniture and rather sombre pictures, a pair of ornate double doors, a nicely modulated murmur of voices, and a woman standing there waiting for me. Young middle-aged and fragile, blue-rinsed hair and a pair of glasses hanging round her neck on a fine chain; all apparently Dresden china, though I doubted it.

"Mr. Hedley," she said. "So kind of you; and so nice to see you. Do come in."

As I followed her into the room there was a sudden silence; all of them looking at me as I stared back at them. It only lasted for a second, but it was unpleasant; and it might have been my over-active imagination again, but they all seemed unreal, as if every one of them was somebody else. One, who could only be Mrs. Messina-Silvestro, like a female counterpart of one of the ancient, hook-nosed Doges; a small, plump rather dowdy old lady who bore an extraordinary resemblance to Queen Victoria, and a girl who could well have been a Botticelli model; pure Renaissance except for her clothes. Another woman who must have been an ex-colonial governor's lady; d'Espinal a head above most of them, still like a Roman emperor in spite of his dinner-jacket and black tie; one other man who looked like nothing so much as a bad-tempered cockatoo and another girl, the youngest of all of them, not more than eighteen, with a pure, beautiful Madonna face. The only two who seemed to be normal were a smart, high-ranking officer of carabiniere in uniform, and a rather serenely handsome dark woman in her early thirties.

At least I knew that one, or I remembered her. A girl at that time, years back in Paris, and a curious name: Emilia Pentecost. She smiled at me and then, as they say, the spell was broken. The momentary illusion of a frozen charade vanished as Celia van Druyten announced, "Amelita, here is Mr. Hedley," the cool voice slightly brittle now, and the old lady said, "Well, Mr. Hedley, now you have appraised us all, what do you think?"

It was a bad start, and to cover it I bowed over her hand. This is regarded as a quaint little affection these days, but I have a dear old friend in France who always expects such attentions, and it did no harm here.

There was the hint of a smile at the corners of her rather thin mouth. She said, "We have been given to understand that you like to pick and choose your subjects, Mr. Hedley. So it is doubly good of you to come so quickly; at an ugly old woman's request."

Manny Levin again, playing hard to get I thought, wondering what he had let me in for this time. Probably a battle of wills, although I would hardly need to paint this portrait at all. It would come out on the canvas by itself; the autocrat, the ageless Italian matriarch looking out at a world which she disliked and despised. I forgot what I answered. Something trite and conventional about it being my privilege, but Celia van Druyten cut in, "Mr. Hedley will have to work very fast?"

"Why?" the old lady asked. "Do you expect me to die? Mr. Hedley will work exactly as he pleases. That is my wish." She gave me the half hint of a smile again. "And as I see him it would make very little difference if it were not."

The atmosphere was getting awkward; a sort of general catching of breath, but this time d'Espinal joined in. "You're going to get on famously together." He seemed to be relieved. "My dear fellow, allow me to add my thanks."

For what? I wondered. Just for coming here or for making a minor and probably temporary hit with the old lady. But there were two more arrivals with the butler at the door, and she said, "You will see that we cannot talk now, Mr. Hedley. Come tomorrow about eleven; if that suits you. We will discuss our arrangements then. Between ourselves." I saw the carabiniere officer frame just one word with his lips to the van Druyten woman, "*Ostinata*", and she shrugged as Mrs. Messina turned away to meet the new arrivals, saying, "Sir Harcourt, introduce Mr. Hedley to our friends."

He was pouting slightly, a fleeting impression of Nero about to do something petulant. "The woman's quite impossible," he murmured. "But you handled her as to the manner born, my dear fellow. You're going to be a great success. Introductions now. A bore, but not so boring as usual, I hope."

The little old lady resembling Queen Victoria turned out just as improbably to be a Princess Kodaly, speaking with a strong Yorkshire accent, and the Botticelli girl with her was Simone Greenwood; pleasant and friendly, but somewhat remote. Professor Venturi, the cockatoo man, somehow attached to the Accademia. He informed me that he did not like modern painters, and I said, "Neither do I; or very few of them." The Governor's lady was Mrs Judith Teestock, kindly but worried about something; as they all were in one way or another. And Emilia Pentecost, wearing a caftan dress in muted peacock greens and blues. She smiled at me again. "Hallo, Paul. It's a long time since the Boul' Mich'. Saturnine as ever, I see. But you look very well. Success suits you."

I said, "If success suits people, Emilia, you must be very successful." The last time I saw Emilia she had been a copyist in the Louvre, and hag-ridden with a miserable love affair; and I had been worse than hard up myself. "What are you doing now?"

She glanced at d'Espinal, and it was difficult to see whether there was malice or affection in it; perhaps a touch of both. "Very little. Nothing really. Trailing in Harry's clouds of glory."

D'Espinal pouted once more. "Come now, my dearest, that's hardly fair to either of us." He appeared to know already that Emilia and I had met before. He turned to the Madonna-faced girl. "Ah, Hedley. Angela Caterina."

She certainly was a beauty. I have always held that there are only two main types of classical beauty; the

Nefertiti and the Madonna, and I realised now that this girl had something of both—except that she was a golden blonde with brown, almost amber eyes. And very quiet; a quiet smile, and a quiet murmur, "How do you do, Mr Hedley." And deceptive, I thought; somebody was going to have trouble with Angela Caterina sooner or later. And Emilia Pentecost hated her.

Celia van Druyten's cool voice again came as a relief. "Mr Hedley, Mrs Messina wants you to meet some of our Venice in Danger Committee.'

All impressions, and apparently far removed from the nonsense with Judith Harford that morning, but they made me uneasy. I listened to the talk about the attempt to save the city, the corrosive pollution creeping over from the oil terminals at Mestre and Marghera, and promised to go to a concert in the cortile of the Ducal Palace in aid of the funds. The Princess Kodaly said, "Come and have a cup of tea with us one of the days, lad." Carson contrived to indicate that he approved of me in the manner best known to butlers; he murmured, "I've got a drop of very proper Scotch if you'd sooner 'ave it." Angela Caterina disappeared; Mrs Teestock looked worried. And it was another relief when she and Emilia Pentecost caught d'Espinal's eye, and he nodded. I took my own leave of Miss van Druyten and Mrs Messina, rewarded by the thin smile again, this time faintly mischievous, was reminded about eleven o'clock tomorrow, and followed them down the stairs.

They had their own motor-boat at the quay, and d'Espinal said, "Can we put you across to the Lido, Hedley? It's on our way. Where the devil is Angela?" he asked.

Emilia was impatient. "Leave her. She'll make her own way back. She always does."

"But it gets so late, dear," Mrs Teestock started. "There are such *very* peculiar people coming to Venice now." She looked at me. One did not discuss family difficulties before strangers. "Mr Hedley, you must come out to San Giorgio when you have time."

"Of course he must." Emilia shivered suddenly. "It's getting quite cool. We can't go searching for her now, Harry. Paul, are you coming?"

It was one of those opalescent, blue-washed evenings that one only gets in Venice, and I said, "I think I'll stay on this side for a bit. Take a walk around."

They did not try to persuade me, and I waited until their motors coughed and the boat nosed off down the canal and then turned back the other way. The two carabinieri were still there, and they watched me as I crossed a bridge to the other side. I was in a little tunnel then, dim in the twilight, and I was not all that surprised by the glimmer of a pale dress and golden hair, the flawless face; and Angela Caterina saying, "Hallo again. I thought it might be worth waiting. My God, that party was drear."

"You shouldn't have done that," I told her mildly. "They're worried about you."

"Like hell they are. Aunt Teestock maybe. But that's only because she's been conditioned. She's still living in Days of Empire. 'One sees such *very* peculiar people in Venice lately.' "

It was a wicked imitation, and I have occasional old-fashioned streaks; I do not much like the young these days. I did not like Angela Caterina at all. "They weren't such bad days. You've been brainwashed yourself."

She laughed. "Dearest Emilia would thank God if I never turned up again. And Sir d'Espinal has been thinking for a long time that I'm one of his mistakes. One of his very few mistakes."

"So you're a poor little misunderstood waif."

She did another astonishing imitation. A begging child's whine. "You wanna buy postcards, signor? You wanna good guide to Venice? I got a pretty sister."

"So that makes two of you."

She laughed again. "You know what I thought? I thought you might be fun."

"I have to have my moments. I don't happen to have one just now."

"We could go to Harry's Bar."

"Harry's Bar would be even less fun."

We were getting out of the quieter streets then, working round towards the Merceria, not quite so solid as it would be in a few weeks, but already packed with strolling crowds between the shops. It was rather more difficult for her there, but she was still game. "No, but we could talk." She was urged aside by a porter pushing a trolley stacked with baggage and chanting "*Permesso*", but she came back again. "I could tell you things."

"I'll bet you could. You might shock me. I've led a sheltered life."

She was shouldered away once more, but still came back fighting and getting angry. "I thought you could easily be a bastard too. You don't even have to try very hard, do you?"

"It comes quite naturally to me."

We were in the Orologio now, working down towards the archway and the sottoportico at the bottom end of St. Mark's Square by the cathedral, more crowds there under the floodlights; and I was getting irritated myself. But I was beginning to doubt my own judgement too. I would defy any normal man to look at that Nefertiti face in the soft ambience of lamplight in St. Mark's Square and still know which of his instincts to trust. In sheer self-defence I said, "Listen, cookie. I'm just here to do a job. That's all. I'm a workman and I like to eat. So that means I don't get involved."

"All right. If that's the way you want it." It was a rejected little girl suddenly, a disappointed little pout. "You might come as far as the Molo with me. I'll get a boat there." She mimicked Mrs Teestock again. "There are some *very* peculiar people in Venice."

The Molo is the main waterfront, as old and as brilliant as history and still one of the great spectacles of the world. I nodded, and we turned off under the glittering mosaics of St. Mark's. Then, just as suddenly, she was stupendously naïve. "I've got plenty of money myself, you know. Or I shall have."

"That's nice for you. So I'll tout for orders. When I've finished Mrs Messina-Silvestro's portrait I'll do one for you."

"Will you?" She stopped again, excited. "Is that a promise? My God, that would make Emilia furious."

"Let's try not to make anybody furious, shall we?"

"Least of all Miss Emilia Pentecost. You know she set you up for this, don't you? She suggested it to Sir d'Espinal."

"Did she? So she did me a favour. Like I said, I have to eat."

"I'm trying to tell you things, you know. And I could tell you a lot more if I wanted to. For instance, you shouldn't let yourself be taken in by that big act of Mrs Messina-S. Underneath it she's a very frightened old woman."

"No," I said decisively. "She doesn't like what she sees around her. But she's certainly not frightened of it."

"That's what you think. She's got reason to be frightened too. And I'll tell you another thing. She's supposed to be immensely wealthy, but she's not. She's given most of it away to save dear wonderful, beautiful Venice. She's crazy. Personally I wouldn't give a damn if the whole place fell down any minute; everybody says it's going to anyway. And all that work she's having done on the house is costing millions."

"Good luck to her then," I said.

"She's going to need it. And so are you."

"So let's hope we get it. Now tell me about San Giorgio," I suggested.

"Damn San Giorgio. It's a little private island away out in the lagoon towards Torcello; Isola San Giorgio Piccolo. It's the Teestock's property. They all think it's heavenly. I can't wait to get away from it fast enough."

We were down at the Molo now, and there was one of the shiny glass cabin-boats picking up expensive tourists for the Muncipal Casino on the Lido. "I'll catch that." She was slightly childish again; petulant and spoiling the flawless face. "I thought I could get *anybody* if I really tried. You're a fool, Mr Paul Hedley. I wanted to be nice to you. I could have been very nice."

"To bad," I said, watching her run aboard and seeing the other passengers turn automatically to stare at her. It was too late then to hope for dinner at the Pensione Martinelli and I turned back to the square to go and sit at Florian's and give myself another drink, several more drinks, watching the crowds drift by under the arcades and wondering which was the real Angela Caterina. There probably wasn't one yet. When a sophisticated young woman is struggling to emerge from the child and knows she's beautiful anything can happen. I felt depressed and oddly on my own. There were too many women in it. I'm starting to get old, and I drink too much, I thought, and went to look for a restaurant.

I cought the last ferry back to the Lido, leaning on the rail and watching the lights drift backwards until they became a long string of glinting jewels laid out on black velvet. It was a dark night, and the glow from the boat spread out all round us like a sort of floating halo pricked here and there by the red lamps on piles marking the sand-banks; which are supposed to be another danger to the city, rising higher every year and deflecting the currents. We seemed to be late; for the opposite number, the last crossing from Santa Elizabetta to San Marco, passed us well before we were halfway over; another blaze of lights passing, with hardly anybody on board.

It seemed darker still after that, and we could not have been more than a few hundred yards out from the Lido landing-stage when I caught sight of the balloons. For a minute I thought I was dreaming or seeing things; for a moment, in fact, I was half panicked. I thought this damned surrealism was starting to get me down. But they were real enough. Some of the other passengers had seen them and were coming to the rail, apparently thinking they were a good comic effect; something to liven up an otherwise uninteresting trip. They were some distance away and only half visible, but you could just make them out straining on their strings, which seemed to be attached to something like a log half in the water. Then they bobbed away idiotically into the darkness.

When we bumped in to the landing-stage the other passengers went on their way. But the ferry captain seemed to have seen more than they had, for he was already shouting down to a group of motor-boats; unidentified objects floating at night in the busiest part of the lagoon are never welcome. A minute later two of them went out with a roar, their headlights swinging over the water, and I waited.

It did not take them long. They came back with the balloons bobbing and bouncing behind them, and when they lifted the sodden bundle out I just got close enough to see that the strings were either tied or entangled round one of his ankles. One brief look at him was quite enough. It was Luigi Antonello the balloon seller. Still the disillusioned monkey face; now a very dead disillusioned monkey with a strand of dark brown seaweed trailing out of its mouth. But it was the balloons which seemed to be the most grotesque feature, bouncing and bobbing above him with a sort of life of their own, the only touch of colour in a harsh black and white picture. One of the boatmen got himself entangled with them and cursed suddenly, muttering, "*Momento; attendere*," and asking for a knife. A second later the balloons shot up into the air, disappearing above the lights; and somehow that seemed to be grotesque too.

There was a crowd gathering from nowhere, with the inevitable pair of carabinieri arriving, and I backed out quickly and crossed the wide road to turn down towards Marco's.

He was just about closing for the night and rather less enthusiastic than usual about seeing me. He said, "That bum Antonello was waiting for you a while. I caught him as he came along and told him a signor wanted him. I told him you pay well." I gathered that he had not much cared for the man sitting at one of his tables on the sidewalk; he seemed to think that his balloons let the tone of the place down, but he shrugged. "It's trade. He was drinking good. He must be in the money. You can bet he'll be here tomorrow."

I rather doubted it, but I said, "Yes. Get me a Scotch, Marco. And have one yourself."

When he brought the drinks he asked, "You still want that bell-boy from the Grand?"

I said, "I don't know. Let it wait a bit."

I did not like anything about today; not even Miss Judith Harford's remark that painters sometimes lead dissolute lives. I do not like anything which starts comic and then turns menacing.

THREE

Before going across to Venice the next morning I called Manny Levin from my room at the pensione. The Martinelli was a small place, with the sort of quiet simplicity some people are prepared to pay a lot for, and the bedroom telephones were one of its few concessions to modernity. I had the impression that the Martinellis themselves rather disapproved of them even, but the daughter who worked the switchboard got my call through promptly enough; and I could only hope that she did not catch any of the conversation.

Manny was still just as keen. He said, "So what gives, Pol?"

"It's hard to say yet. Several things by the look of it; and they may or may not be connected. I think they are. It's got something to do with Venice itself. Pollution. The foundations rotting; the place sinking, and so on. There's a lot of local politics about that.

And there seems to be a monstrous regiment of women involved. Including Queen Christina of Sweden."

It sounded screwy again, I thought; and so did Manny. He enquired, "Are you nuts, Pol?"

"That's always a possibility. But if I remember bits of my history Christina was quite a girl. Didn't she once sell a collection of pictures which technically wasn't her property? You might look up the references to find out whether any of them have gone missing since then."

Manny went quiet for a minute, working that one out. I could almost hear him thinking round it before he murmured, "I see. Or I think I see. How did you home in on that?"

"A Miss Judith Harford. Another of the monstrous regiment, but what anybody would call a very nice girl. Do you happen to have any contacts in Boston, Massachusetts?"

He thought about that too. "I might have."

"Get on to them today to see if anybody knows anything about her. It's a long shot, but it might pay off." I told him about Judith Harford, but did not mention the balloon seller. After last night I felt that the less said about Antonello the better; especially on the telephone. "It was just a chance meeting and a rather inconsequential conversation. All of it at tangents. But when I told her I was a painter she latched on. And when Mrs Messina-Silvestro's name came up she brought in Queen Christina of Sweden out of the blue. And then waited to see whether there was a reaction. When there wasn't she lost interest."

"Too bad," Manny said sympathetically. "A nice girl like that. See now, Pol, are you sure she wasn't out looking for you?"

"Why should she be? I've told you, that was entirely accidental. But if you do get any information I'd like it as soon as possible. I wouldn't go so far as to say that our Miss Harford is too innocent for this wicked world, but I do have a feeling that she might find herself up against something she can't handle."

"Your intuition again, is it, Pol?"

He was quite serious, and I said, "It could be; some of it. I just don't like the atmosphere." And other things, I thought.

The time was getting on, and I rather hurriedly told him a bit about Mrs Messina-Silvesgro's party. Then he asked, "Have you heard anything of Hans Kleber yet?"

"The Munich expert? Not so far. I don't want to ask direct questions."

"No. Maybe that's wise. But I'd like to know if he's really there, Pol. If he is it's something very, very big. All right then; if I find anything I'll call you back about ten tonight. How does it look for the portrait now?"

I said , "That's no problem. The old lady will paint that herself. All I have to do is get it on the canvas."

There was nothing very much about the first session with Mrs Messina-Silvestro—there rarely is for a first sitting—except that they sent their own boat for me again, and there were still two carabinieri not far from the house. Carson admitted me, without the aroma of cloves this time, but otherwise with something more than a hint of merely polite recognition in his eye. Celia van Druyten did not appear, but Mrs Messina was waiting for me, and the rest of it was mostly making arrangements, explaining how I liked to work, and getting down a few preliminary soft pencil sketches. All quite normal and even rather dull; but it was quite clear that I was not going to have anything to complain about, and d'Espinal had advised on the room with the best light at this time of day and sent over an impressive easel from San Giorgio. This was a highly professional German made affair with all sorts of gadgets for tilting and lifting the canvas, and it had seen a great deal of use recently; so, since so far as I know d'Espinal himself did not do any painting, it looked as if Emilia Pentecost had been very busy for some time past.

Rather curiously the easel caused the only odd note at that sitting. The old lady was still slightly autocratic, but obviously enjoying herself; and if she was frightened of something, as Angela Caterina had said, I saw no sign of it. We arranged that she would give me an hour every morning from Mondays to Fridays, while I was free to come earlier or stay later to work on without her if it suited me, and then she got on to technicalities. Sitters often want to know how it is done, and I told her that I preferred to use a limited palette and fairly direct colour. "Quite solid," I said. "Quite different from whoever's been using this easel lately, for instance. Most painters leave their trademarks," I went on. "And if it's Miss Pentecost she's been using a lot of transparent glazes. You can see where she's wiped her brushes out on the wood. Has she been experimenting with some of the early Italian techniques?"

At that time I did not connect Emilia with anything. I was just mildly inquisitive, wondering what she was doing these days, but it produced an unmistakable reaction. You could feel the frost in the air; and Mrs Messina-Silvestro could administer a snub like a kick from a mule. "I have no idea. No doubt if Miss Pentecost wishes you to discuss her work she will invite you to do so herself." There was an awkward pause, and to have apologised would merely have made matters worse. I went on with the last light sketch I was rubbing in as if I had not noticed anything, and then soon afterwards she asked, "Shall we say that is enough for today?"

Carson was summoned to see me out, and the

atmosphere thawed slightly when she looked over the sketches. In fact she was as delighted as a schoolgirl with them, although she did her best not to show it. She said, "Not flattering; but you make me look quite *interesting*, Mr Hedley. Shall we say tomorrow at eleven again?" So I was warned and reprieved, but when Carson was marching majestically ahead of me along the corridor he did that trick of floating something on the air without apparently moving his lips. "Wot's upset her?"

I was glancing at the pictures as we passed them, and I waited until we were on the stairs to the lower hall, where there were half a dozen workmen busy. "I've no idea. A rather tactless question I think. How did you know?"

"Ah," he breathed. "Questions. They're best not asked, ain't they? She gets a sort of tight-lipped look. She's worried; see?" He looked at the workmen disapprovingly. "All this mess, and one thing and another. She shouldn't never have started it." But when we got to the massive double doors on the canal he was back to butlering again. "At what hour shall I send the motor-boat for you tomorrow?"

I stared at him. "The same time, if you want to. D'you mean to say you're going to send it every day?"

"Mrs Messina-Silvestro has given instructions that you are to have every facility, sir."

"Yes," I said. "It's very kind." Then I tried Carson's own trick, speaking almost inaudibly. "Is there any place you go for a drink in your off-duty hours?"

His eyes were roving up and down the quay, at the workmen out here preparing to knock off for their midday break, at the two carabinieri now leaning on the bridge, at a water-taxi nosing in to the steps. "Benito's in the Calle della Fava, most nights after nine o'clock," he murmured; and then added, "Watch it."

Celia van Druyten was stepping out of the taxi. "Mr

Hedley," she cried. "So nice. I wanted to catch you before you left. Carson, pay the man for me, will you? Did you have a good morning, Mr Hedley?"

There was an odd look in Carson's small eyes. There was no love lost there, I thought briefly, but I said, "Very good, thank you. One couldn't wish for a better sitter."

"I'm so glad. Carson never tips them so heavily as I do," she whispered. "We have to be careful. What I wanted to say, Mr Hedley. . . We all want you to be as quick as possible. We want to get Mrs Messina-Silvestro away." She made a little gesture with one hand, taking in the building work, the workmen and scaffolding, and perhaps also the two carabinieri. "All this. The noise and the dust. It's so bad for her, but she's so obstinate. You mustn't tire her, of course; but please try to get it done as quickly as possible. You do understand, don't you?"

"Yes," I said. "I do understand." Or did I, I wondered.

There were two fresh surprises waiting for me at the Martinelli. One decidedly unpleasant and the other perhaps slightly dubious. The first was a fresh officer of carabiniere waiting for me in the reception. I do not know anything about Italian police organisation, except that there seem to be several sorts of them, and that the carabinieri seem to be by far the most sinister. This was a young man, younger than myself, apparently of a higher rank than those one sees on the streets, but not so high as the one at Mrs Messina's party last night. He was smart and looked unpleasantly intelligent; he spoke fluent English, even with an affection of slightly outdated slanginess, and he was obviously very keen. "Signor Hedley?" he started. "Sorry to descend on you like this, just on lunch-time as it is. But could we have the odd word or two?"

"Why not?" But Martinelli's pretty daughter was watching us with considerable interest, and I asked, "Is it private? Or shall we go into the lounge?"

He was all friendliness. "Oh, the lounge of course." Fortunately the place was empty, most of the few guests now congregating on the terrace for lunch, and I waited for him. "A bit of a dodgy incident last night," he explained. "A fellow fished out of the lagoon. A bit of a undesirable character named Antonello. Tied up to a string of balloons, of all things."

"Very odd," I said.

"Very. The captain of the last *vaporetto* coming over from San Marco spotted it."

I reckoned out quickly how much to tell him. It was just possible that I had been seen and might be described. I said, "So that's what it was? If it's any help to you I was on that ferry and I saw the balloons myself. At first I thought somebody must have lost them, but when they sent the boats out I waited for a few minutes and watched them bring him in."

"You did? That's fine. So can you say whether the balloons were actually tied to his ankle or whether he was simply tangled up with them?"

I shook my head. "I can't, I'm afraid. I didn't get that close. To tell you the truth I'd had a rather rich dinner and quite a drink or two. I didn't think the sight would be all that good for my stomach."

"Very natural. The trouble is nobody else seems to know either. The damn fool who pulled him into the boat says the things were a nuisance and he cut the string. He won't swear to anything either way."

And faced with this keen young character I could well understand it, I thought. I asked, "Does it make much difference?"

"Oh' yes. The devil of a lot. You see he was full to the back teeth with alcohol. It's just possible that he did get tangled. And the rails on those ferries are dangerously low. If he was leaning over it's just possible again that the wind on those damned balloons could have finished the trick and overbalanced him. On the other hand if they were actually tied to his ankle they'd just lift his legs enough to keep his head under water. You see what I mean? Ingenious, really; you couldn't think of a better way of drowning anybody."

"I prefer not to try. Was he on that ferry then? The one crossing from this side?"

"Again we can't be sure. There were very few people on it anyway, and we haven't traced anybody who saw him. Not even the rail-hand. He was in the upper deck bar having a quick final drink." He grinned at me disarmingly. "Against the rules, of course, but they all do it on the last trip."

I said, "I suppose they do. It's unfortunate."

"Very." He paused for a second. "Did you happen to get close enough to recognise him?"

There was a wicked little catch there. I said, "Not really. The balloons caught my attention more.. Then there was a crowd round almost at once. I've never believed in standing about at an accident when you can't do anything."

"And you weren't feeling too good yourself." He was pleasantly sympathetic. "So, there it is. It's a damn nuisance though; and very odd. He'd got a lot of money on him, f'instance. Over twenty-five thousand lire. And as I said, he was a decidedly shady character. We've suspected for some time that he was up to his eyes in drug peddling. Maybe the hard stuff, and certainly khiff. Marihuana," he explained kindly. "You call it pot, don't you?"

For God's sake, I thought, not drugs as well as everything else, and he went on, "It worries the hotel managements stiff. The gilded little boys and girls over here, you know. And the other sort; the drop-outs. Well," he finished, "I mustn't keep you from your lunch any longer. It's been nice meeting you, Mr Hedley."

Then he pulled a mean, sneaky little trick; the sort of trick I should have tried myself had I been doing his job. He'd put on his cap and was turning to leave before he stopped again. "There is this other little thing though." When he turned back to me he had that sketch I had done at Marco's bar in his hand. He sounded almost apologetic this time. "That's why I asked if you might have recognised him."

I could only hope I was keeping a poker face; and although the answer was obvious, quietly cursing Marco to myself but not really blaming him, I asked, "Where did you get that?" to give myself time.

He was still slightly apologetic. "One of our chaps spotted Antonello at Marco's bar last night, so I had to go along and have a word or two myself. It's peculiar though, don't you think? A sort of coincidence is it?"

I had to think fast. The choice lay between telling him that I wanted to know why Antonello was following Judith Harford and who was paying for it, or simply putting up a reasonably plausible story; and I had no means of knowing which was the right one. But the reference to drugs worried me, while the Harford girl would scarcely thank me for putting the police on to question her; and that might spoil any chance I had myself of finding out what she was after here. It might have been a mistake, but I said, "It is. Just a coincidence. But otherwise really quite simple."

I explained what I was doing in Venice, and I thought there was a momentary reaction of some sort when I mentioned Mrs Messina-Silvestro, but he did not say anything, and I went on, "I often make sketches of any odd types I happen to see. Almost everybody in my trade does. It's a habit. And I've got a vague idea of doing a whole series of them while I'm here; Venetian characters. I thought this one might be worth working up. You know the sort of thing; give him a couple of thousand lire and get him to stand about for an hour or so."

"Yes. . ." he murmured. "I see." And I had no means of knowing how far he was convinced either. "But I'd hardly call him a Venetian type. More Arabic, I'd say. It's good though; really very good. Do you mind if I keep it?" Apparently it would not have made much difference if I had said I did. It was already going back into the pocket of his immaculate jacket. "Now Mrs Messina-Silvestro really is Venetian. You might even call her one of our ancient momuments. Do you know, if she ever wanted to leave Venice I don't believe we'd let her go. We've got a thing about works of art, you know." He looked at his wrist-watch. "Good Lord, is that the time? I really must be on my way."

As if I had been keeping him I thought sourly, seeing him out through the reception, and turning back to go through to the terrace and my next surprise; the dubious one. Miss Judith Harford herself; sitting halfway through her lunch and at my table.

"I hope it's a pleasant surprise," she enquired.

I said, "Very."

"You don't look as if it is. But perhaps you take your pleasures seriously. I made up my mind quite on the spur of the moment. I was walking past here this morning, and I thought, 'My, what a *sweet* little place; and what *very* good taste Mr Hedley must have.' And with me to think is to act. My family say I'm sometimes *too* impulsive. I took a taxi straight back to the Quattro Fontane, collected my baggage, and here I am."

I stared at her. "D'you mean you're staying here?"

"Indeed I am."

"Why?"

"Why not?" She was sweetly reasonable. "I like it. I did not like the Quattro Fontane all that much. It was quite expensive and so. . ." She did another brilliant little hand gesture and thought-projection impressions; the gilded youth, a flock of chattering parakeets and a touch of discotheque.

"Quite," I said.

"And it's such a peaceful street. The trees; and those pretty little villas, and that little canal. Do you realise that that canal is barely more than six inches deep. Isn't that surprising?"

"Mind-boggling. But that's supposed to be good for you, isn't it? I once read somewhere that you should always try to boggle your mind at least once every day."

She looked at me rather severely. "I don't think you're *really* being quite serious. Did you have a pleasant morning? And what was your first impression of Mrs Messina-Silvestro?"

So now we're getting to the real business, I thought. "That was mind-boggling too."

She sighed faintly. "I have a growing feeling that conversation with you might easily get very, very odd."

I nodded. "I don't have a family, but that's what my friends say too."

There was a pause while I ordered, and then she chose to throw her next bombshell. "Did you have an interesting talk with that *charming* lootenant?"

I stopped dead in my study of the menu and stared at her again, a horrible suspicion crossing my mind. "How do you know he's a lieutenant?"

"Because he told me. Lootenant Alberti."

It was a peaceful atmosphere. There was nothing to indicate what she had exploded. A quiet German family at one table; an elderly French gentleman with the ribbon of the Legion of Honour in his buttonhole, both he and his rather severe wife eating with thoughtful concentration; a young couple obviously on honeymoon and concentrating more on each other; a plump and placid lady, a comfortable-looking priest, and a beautiful Russian Blue cat sitting on the wall and surveying us all benevolently. It was not the sort of scene in which lieutenants of carabiniere and rather unpleasantly drowned balloon sellers should have had any part at all; but I asked helplessly, "Did you talk to him?"

"Of course I talked to him. Why, he'd been to the Quattro Fontane and then came on here when they told him I'd moved over. It seems that two of his men saw us in the Viale Elizabetta yesterday when you made that dreadful scene with the balloon man."

That took my breath away again for a minute and I missed the next bit, but she went on, "He wanted to know if the man ever offered to sell me anything, and I asked him did I *look* the kind of person who would want to buy a big red balloon, and he agreed that I certainly do not; then he asked if the man had said anything to me at all, and I told him he had not but I surely said plenty to him. Or I would have done if you had not started what very nearly came up to a street brawl."

And obviously I had picked exactly the wrong story to tell the lieutenant. I said, "A woman with a long tongue is a flight of steps leading to calamity."

"What was that?" Miss Harford enquired dangerously.

"I was quoting an ancient Chinese proverb. It goes on, 'For disaster is not sent from Heaven, but is brought about on earth by women.' "

The green sparks were beginning to flash again. "I do not think that is very nice, Mr Hedley. But I would say it is one of your very *favourite* proverbs."

"It is," I agreed. "Did the lieutenant tell you

anything about Antonello?"

"He did not. Except that he is a most undesirable person. And it is unlikely that I shall be bothered any more by him."

"I should think it's extremely unlikely," I agreed again. I decided there was no need to tell her about a particularly unpleasant way of drowning balloon sellers. "Let's concentrate on our lunch, shall we?" I said.

"I have nearly finished mine. And I must say rather thankfully."

"Come with me to Murano this afternoon," I suggested.

"Have you any particular reason for going to Murano?" she asked.

"Only to take you."

"Then thank you very much. It's *very* kind of you. But I think I'll just sit here on the terrace and read."

It was a pity, I thought. And, oddly enough, I felt that she was just as disappointed as I was myself.

I went to Murano anyway, and it was tired, dusty and sad. The glass museum was tired, dusty and sad too; the cathedral of San Donato, where there is a mosaic I wanted to see, was closed; and the glass-making was clever but hardly worth the trouble. The only item of interest was an inoffensive young man in a brown linen suit. He was on the boat coming out; he appeared conscientiously wherever I went; he was on the boat going back, and he appeared conscientiously again when I walked down the Viale Elizabetta to Marco's. He looked very bored, and I could quite understand it.

Marco was reproachful, but defensive. He muttered, "See now, signore, you're here for two, maybe three weeks. I'm here all my life, and I have to make my living."

"I quite understand, Marco," I said. "There's no

harm done. We hope."

He seemed to want to make it up to me somehow. "I can still get that bell-boy from the Grand."

"Better not." But then I had an afterthought. "No, wait. There's something you might do for me yourself, Marco. It's worth a couple of thousand. Just ask him if they have a Dr Hans Kleber of Munich staying there."

There did not seem to be anything else I could do, and I went back to the Martinelli for dinner, but there was no sign of Miss Harford. I wondered if she had had another impulsive fit and moved on again, although I did not really think so because it was quite obvious now that she wanted something; and the Martinelli who served as waiter told he she had advised them that she would be dining out tonight. He appeared to imagine there was a budding romance somewhere. "A very nice lady," he said sympathetically. "*Gentile*. It is disappointing, eh?"

After that I considered going across to Venice to pick up Carson. I had a feeling that he might tell me things, and I could shake off Brown Linen easily enough if I tried. But on the other hand I wanted to be here to take Manny Levin's telephone call, and it might be difficult to get back in time. In the end I settled for a long aimless walk along the Riviera San Nicolò, with Venice glittering in the twilight across the lagoon, and then back to Marco's to sit and watch the late evening promenade. Brown Linen was still there, getting very bored indeed now; and I was getting puzzled. I would have thought that Lieutenant Alberti was far too subtle and intelligent to do anything as obvious as that.

Manny came through just after ten, and he was still excited. "I don't have much about Queen Christina of Sweden for you yet. I've got a research agency on it, and they think it might take a day or two. It seems there were quite a lot of pictures involved. But I've a very fascinating word from Boston about your girlfriend."

"Don't let your imagination run away with you, Manny," I told him. "She's just a nice girl."

"Yes? Well maybe she is. The word I have is that she is also a *Doctor* Judith Harford, and the world's youngest leading expert on. . . Guess who?"

Manny likes a little dramatic touch occasionally, and I let him have it. "I couldn't even start. Who?"

"It's getting bigger than I thought, Pol. Leonardo da Vinci."

"Yes," I agreed. "That is big."

"And there's more about the lady herself. From what I gather even tough and hardened old professors run screaming for cover when they see Dr Judith Harford bearing down on them. How does that strike you?"

"As you say. Fascinating."

He was serious suddenly. "Be careful, Pol. I can see a bit of what it may be. And it could be very dangerous."

I said, "Yes. I'm starting to get the same sort of idea myself. Believe me, Manny, I mean to be very careful."

I was vaguely uneasy about the reception switchboard, and I did not say anything about Antonello or the lieutenant, and after a few minutes more we cut off. Then the night was still fairly young and I walked slowly across to the Casino; it would give Brown Linen something to do I thought. He was sitting patiently on a bench by the side of the canal, and he followed me just as patiently. When I got there and went upstairs to the roulette-room he was almost on my heels, and after that he kept fairly close to me. He did not play himself—I imagine his expenses did not cover roulette—but he watched me playing, and I lost. It was the only time I saw him looking interested or amused.

I am a believer in luck, or rather I believe in states of mind which encourage luck or otherwise, and I never go on playing when I am obviously on a losing streak. I left the Casino just before eleven-thirty and turned to the left, intending to walk back comfortably to the Viale, and then invite Brown Linen to have a nightcap with me. The Lungomare Marconi is a wide, straight road illuminated by quite widely spaced sodium vapour lamps, which seemed to cast alternate pools of orange light and shadow, and at this time of the night surprisingly deserted although it was still comparatively early for the Lido; a car flaring past now and then, but nobody else walking, the darkness of the sands and sea on my right, and gardens on this side. This way also would bring me past the Grand Hotel, five minutes or so further on; and that was an additional thought. I had a fairly obvious idea that this was where Dr Judith came for her lunch- and dinner-dates.

It was a thousand-to-one chance against meeting her, of course. She should have been safely back at the Martinelli by now. But as it happened the thousandth chance came up. I caught sight of her coming out of the main park gates of the hotel with a man, something more than a hundred yards away. In that light it was difficult to make out very much, but he appeared to be middle-aged, wearing a small imperial beard and a dinner-jacket; and they seemed to be arguing. I thought of Manny Levin's remark that even hardened old professors ran screaming when they saw Dr Judith Harford bearing down on them, and the man turned back abruptly through the gates. She had a light evening-coat over her shoulders and this swung out as she turned too, now coming towards me, obviously taking the shortest way back to the pensione. Then I saw something which she could not see. Another man coming out of the hotel grounds behind her, and a big car standing further back only on parking-lights beginning to creep forward.

Anybody could see what that was, and I started to run, thankful to hear Brown Linen pounding behind me. But we were both still too far off, and it drew up beside Judith with one of the passengers in front apparently asking something, for she stopped and bent down innocently to answer. But at the same time the rear door was opening and another one getting out. There was no doubt of him. It was the bearded character on the camera truck, taking shots of us in the Viale Elizabetta the other day. Close behind me now, Brown Linen shouted, and then it all happened at once. Judith stiffened like an outraged spinster; a woman's arm came out of the front window to stop her, the beard tried to catch her shoulders and the coat she was wearing came off in his hands. The man from the hotel grounds came in, the beard tripped him somehow and flung the coat over his head. I reached Judith myself and swung her away across the sidewalk. And I caught a glimpse of a pale, beautiful Nefertiti face in the nearside front seat.

It takes longer to tell than it did to start and finish. The beard shot back into the car, its lights snapped off and the door slammed as it accelerated viciously. Then it was roaring away, and Brown Linen shrugged. I caught sight of a gun in his hand, but it vanished as quickly as the car itself disappeared. "The impudence," Judith breathed, "the very *impudence* of it," and then immediately became Dr Judith Harford again. "You may let me go, Mr Hedley. I am quite capable, thank you." She stared at me accusingly, as if it were my fault somehow. "First they simply enquired the way to the Via Lorenzo Marcello. And then that girl said, 'Would you like to come to a party?' "

Brown Linen shrugged once more. There was some sort of wordless communication passing between himself and the other man. "It could be. These things happen.

The other nodded. "Too often. Young fools, signorina. More money than sense. What do you say? 'Beating it up.' "

If she believed that she would believe anything, I thought. I asked, "Did you get the number of that car?

He looked at me woodenly. "Did you?"

I hadn't, of course. In practice people very rarely do, and it had all been too quick. I said, "Let's go then. It was very kind, gentlemen. If we might know who we have to thank. . ?"

But they were giving nothing away. "It's of no importance, signor. Only fortunate we were here. Perhaps if you will escort the signorina. . ?"

Judith seemed disposed to stop and argue about it, but I repeated, "Let's go," and started her off towards the Viale Elizabetta. She was obviously quite safe now, but I still had an instinct to get her under the brighter lights and in a more populated place. She came quietly for a time, considerably more frightened than she appeared to be, and then she said, "It certainly wasn't a party. But why? And why me?"

"At a guess I'd say that you know something somebody else wants to know," I told her. "And at another guess it could have something to do with Queen Christina of Sweden."

She glanced at me sideways, quickly, but neither was she rising to anything. We were at the corner of the Elizabetta by then, and she looked back over her shoulder instead. "They're still there. Just walking along together behind us. Who are they?"

"If we're lucky they're your nice Lieutenant Alberti's men. I think they are. If they're not, I don't know."

She was starting to get irritable, stopping briefly and staring at me. "That's nonsense. *Why* should the lootenant have men following me? It's quite ridiculous."

"I wish it were. It could have something to do with your balloon man." I should have told her then what had happened to Antonello, and about the drugs angle, but I did not want to add any fresh complications. I said, "That girl in the car. I only caught a quick glimpse of her, and I can't be sure. Would you say she was a Nefertiti or the Madonna type?

Judith stared at me again. "Mr Hedley, is this about to become another of your peculiar conversations? Because if it is let me tell you that I am not in the mood for it. It was certainly a very pretty girl. I would not have stopped else." She seemed to turn suspicious herself suddenly. "And how did *you* come to be there? Were you following me too?"

"I went to the Casino. I was losing. I decided to walk back by way of the Elizabetta. Quite simple."

"Oh dear," she murmured. "I must seem *very* unkind. I would not have you think I'm ungrateful. But I do feel there is something you are not telling me."

"So that makes two of us," I said sourly.

We were back at the Martinelli by then, and the one who served as waiter was doubling as night porter now, beaming all over his face apparently at the thought of the romance starting to bud again. He was just opening the glass doors for us when the reception telephone began to ring stridently, and he said, "Dear God; at this time of night; *scusi*." Judith announced rather coldly that she was going straight up to her room, and I wondered fleetingly whether I might somehow tempt her into mine, whether this was one of those rare occasions when she might be persuaded to take a drink with a dissolute painter, when Martinelli called, "Signor Hedley." He was holding out the receiver with all thoughts of romance banished; distinctly disapproving. "For you."

It said, "'Edley?" and at first I thought it must be Carson; but it was the wrong voice. It struck me as being deliberately coarsened. It asked, "So you got back all right, did you? So listen, mate. Don't yack; just listen. Just keep your bleedin' nose out of our business, will you? If not you might get roughed up a bit. You might get roughed up real bad."

It went off with a click, and I handed the receiver back to Martinelli, who was still obviously registering that he hoped I was not going to make a habit of receiving calls at this hour. "I'm sorry about that," I said. "It was nothing important." Then I went up to my own room and gave myself a Scotch from the bottle I kept there in case of emergencies. I gave myself several, while thinking about a number of things, especially Angela Caterina, and starting to get very angry.

FOUR

If Miss Harford had been frightened by the incident last night she showed no sign of it when I went out to the terrace next morning. She was sitting behind a glass of orange juice, admiringly attended by the youngest and prettiest of the Martinelli girls who always served the breakfasts, and feeding the Russian Blue cat with scraps of Melba toast; which he accepted gracefully, but with no particular enthusiasm. She said, "My, you're late this morning, Mr Hedley."

"I spent a thoughtful night," I told her. "Coffee, please, Graziella."

There was a companiable silence then until the cat transferred his attention to my side of the table, when she asked, "Isn't he beautiful? Do you like cats?"

"I'm always respectful to them."

The look in her eye seemed to be saying, "Then they must be about the only things you are respectful to," but she next enquired kindly, "And what are your plans today?"

"Mrs Messina-Silvestro first. They'll be sending their boat for me sharp at half-past ten."

That did impress her. "They send their boat for you? Every day? My, they are treating you importantly."

"Not really. They send the boat, but they let me find my own way back. The boat and the boatmen are my credentials," I explained. "There are two carabinieri on permanent standby outside the Ca' Messina. I imagine they must get changed periodically. So if I went without the boat any of them who hadn't seen me before would almost certainly stop me and ask who I am. The boat is simply to stop me getting inquisitive and asking embarrassing questions."

"Carabinieri on guard? But why?"

"That would be the embarrassing question, wouldn't it? And at another wild guess," I added carefully, "it might even have something to do with the people who tried to snatch you last night."

But Dr Harford was still giving nothing away. She said, "I think we should forget that incident, Mr Hedley. It was just a silly prank. But it was very, very unpleasant and I do not wish to talk about it any more."

"That's fine," I agreed. "But there might be other people who do." Almost the gift of prophecy if it hadn't been so obvious, I thought, for at that moment little Graziella came out with my coffee, announcing breathlessly, "Signor Hedley; the *telefono*." I said, "And that will be the first."

It was. Lieutenant Alberti; still apparently friendly enough, but with noticeably less of the old school friends together atmosphere. The conversation did not take long, and when I went back to the terrace I said, "The nice lieutenant. He wants to have a word with both of us at the *Questura*; separately. I'm to take you across in the Ca' Silvestro boat, and put you off at San

Marco, where he'll have a man waiting for you. Then it's my turn after I've finished with Mrs Messina at twelve o'clock."

There was a distinct Daughters of the Revolution look developing. "And suppose I refuse to go?"

"I don't think he can make you; not yet. He was quite polite about it, but I had the impression that he's badly worried about something. It would be very, very unsympathetic to say 'Nuts to you, Lieutenant'. And very unwise."

The sitting went well that morning. Whatever I had said yesterday appeared to have been forgotten, or at least forgiven, and the old lady was in an amiable mood. She had settled typically on the most uncompromising of the sketches, the one I should have chosen myself—largely, I gathered, because Celia van Druyten had disliked it—and, as I had expected, the impression started to get itself down on the canvas; nice, free charcoal work to start with. "It's going well," I told myself. "No tactless questions today." But I encouraged her to talk, and she had no inhibitions about asking them; mostly about myself. I told her something about my old friend Rosina Saillens in Monte Carlo, a character not unlike herself, and she said rather maliciously, "You appear to be very successful with old women."

"Mostly because as portraits they're often more interesting than young ones. Although," I added cautiously, "there was an extraordinarily beautiful girl at your party the other night."

"Angela Caterina?" She made a surprising little sound halfway between a sniff and a grunt. "You should not let yourself be fooled."

I could have told her that I was hardly likely to be, but said nothing, and there was a little silence until she went on abruptly, "I am not only an old woman, Mr Hedley; I am also an old-fashioned old woman, and I believe there is such a thing as old-fashioned wickedness. There's bad blood there. So far as anybody can be sure her parents were fisher-folk in Chioggia. Not that I have anything against fishermen. They do a useful work and no doubt most of them are very estimable people. But what's bred in the bone comes out in the flesh. She was a street beggar at one time; here in Venice."

Put like that it sounded like good old-fashioned snobbery to me; but I could see her point. "She seems to have come a long way since then," I murmured non-committally.

There was another pause until Mrs Messina said, "She has indeed. Thanks to Harcourt d'Espinal. It's a curious story. I suspect it was a great deal more curious than most people will ever know.* You have heard of the lost Sleeping Cupid of Michelangelo?"

D'Espinal and missing works of art again, I thought; but still carefully non-committal I asked, "Isn't that the piece that Michelangelo himself forged as an early classical work and then sold to one of the cardinals? There was a considerable scandal about it at the time. Then later Charles the First bought it from the d'Este family; and it has never been seen since."

She inclined her head graciously. "You are really quite well informed. Very well then. Some years ago, and here in Venice, Sir Harcourt d'Espinal discovered this Cupid, or a remarkably fine copy of it—he is reticent about that, as about many other details of the affair—and Angela Caterina was somehow incidental to the discovery. Subsequently he sold the work for a very considerable sum of money, again in somewhat peculiar circumstances, and placed one half of it in trust for the girl."

*The Stone Baby.

"It sounds fascinating," I said. "And it was certainly generous."

"Generous?" Mrs Messina snapped. "In the light of the girl's character it was madness. She runs around *telling* people how wealthy she is; the fisher-folk blood coming out, you see. She is a target for most of the undesirables in Venice. And there are more than enough of them."

We left it at that. The old lady seemed suddenly to feel that she was talking too much, and she was obviously getting tired. It was interesting, I thought, but it was hardly likely to have much bearing on what was happening now; except that it hinted at some of d'Espinal's activities. And I wondered what he or somebody else had discovered more recently.

The conversation with Alberti was on a distinctly different level. It was in a bleak, unpleasant little office in the police building overlooking the Rio di San Lorenzo, and he started in immediately, "You didn't tell me the whole of it yesterday, Mr Hedley, did you? Why not?"

"I wanted to keep Miss Harford out of it if I could. I didn't realise that you'd already spoken to her."

"It's a dirty trick we have. So perhaps you'd better tell me now."

I did not wait for him to press the point, and when I finished he said, "So you did recognise Antonello when they got him out of the water last night. And we still want to know whether those strings were tied around his ankle or just tangled."

"I did recognise him; yes. About the strings, I can't say. That's definite. I didn't get close enough to look. That's definite too. By that time I wanted to keep well out of it myself."

He sat watching me for a minute over his cigarette; intelligent, ambitious, and very badly worried about something. "That's understandable. But you've left it a bit late now, haven't you? You asked Marco to contact him for you. And not because he was just a pretty face. So why?"

"I wanted to find out who'd put him on to mark Miss Harford. The theory being that somebody must have paid him to do the job, and he'd tell me who it was if I offered to pay him more."

"That's reasonable enough. Has it occurred to you that if he was murdered it might have been because he was seen sitting at Marco's bar last night waiting for you? To prevent him telling you?"

"It has crossed my mind. Look," I said, "using a balloon seller to tail anybody seems ludicrous. But it makes sense when you think that he can be seen as a marker in a crowd; by a man with a movie camera for instance. There's a lot of film of Judith Harford somewhere by now; because they meant to get somebody to impersonate her. and thats why they tried to snatch her last night."

"Yes," he murmured. "I've thought of something like that too. But let's get on to last night. She says there were three people in the car. Two men and a very pretty girl; quite young. Can you add anything?"

It might have been another mistake, but I thought Angela Caterina was best forgotten for the present. The connection with d'Espinal and the Ca' Silvestro worried me, and I said, "I can't. Did your men get the number?"

"They didn't. The damn fools. It was a Mercedes. But there are dozens of Mercedes here. And they couldn't even be certain what colour it was."

"Nobody could be certain of colour in that light. And there are even more pretty girls than Mercedes. The Exelsior alone seems to be alive with them. But I think I might help you with one of the men. May I have your scribbling-pad for a minute." I put down a quick sketch of the man with the beard and pushed it back to him, saying, "That's the one who got out of the car. And he was the cameraman in the Viale Elizabetta the other day."

The lieutenant did not seem to think it was one of my best efforts. "It could be anybody. And there must be hundreds of men with beards too."

"Far too many," I agreed. "I've never liked them myself. And they're far too easy to shave off if necessary. But there can't be all that many camera cars or film companies. Do you know of any? Officially?"

"I know of one. But for God's sake they can't be mixed up in this. You'll get me shot if I so much as suggest it. They've got the backing of the Mayor and Municipality; the Venice in Danger Committee; even your Mrs Messina-Silvestro. They're making a film about the erosion; called 'Venice in Crisis', or something like that. Strictly speaking it's up to the Municipal Police to look after them, but everybody's had instructions to give them all the facilities and help they might ask for."

And that might be riddled with local politics, I thought, remembering some of the scraps of conversation heard at the Ca' Silvestro the other night. "Look," I said, "I don't pretend I can tell you how or why, but I've a feeling that Judith Harford's trouble might somehow be connected with the erosion and restoration here. Do you happen to know whether this film they're making is just a documentary or a full feature with a story attached to it?"

He stared at me rather blankly. "I've no idea, I'm afraid. So far I haven't been all that interested, but I suppose I could find out. Does it matter?"

"It might do. If it's a documentary they could be working with just a camera crew and director. If it's a feature they might have very nearly a full company here. Including make-up artists."

"I see," He was far too intelligent not to. "I think I see. But I find it difficult to believe, you know. And if I start treading on important people's toes it could get very tricky."

"Tricky for Miss Harford too. And for me. We haven't yet touched on the phone call I had last night."

I told him about that, and he said, "Yes; unpleasant. But calls like that are not uncommon, you know. Do you take it seriously?"

"Very. I should feel quite justified in asking for protection for both of us."

"My dear chap," he protested. "We haven't the men. And it's never very practical. Or not for long. The best we could do would be to suggest that you and the lady should leave Venice."

"I can't. I wouldn't anyway. And you might just as well try to move the Statue of Liberty as move Judith Harford."

Apparently he had already tried. He was faintly rueful about it. "I rather gathered that. By the way, she left a message. If you're not too late she'll be waiting for you at Florian's."

"That's nice of her." He looked at his watch and I looked at mine; and then when he was opening the door for me I tried his own trick on him. "Another by the way. The man you put on to follow me yesterday was really very obvious. Or was it another one like the balloon seller? Now you've taken him off today I shan't be likely to notice the one who's really tailing me? Or us?"

Just for a second the easy amiability vanished. I caught a glimpse of the ambitious young copper who is out to impress the people upstairs. "He was quite useful last night, wasn't he? Mr Hedley, you're smart and you seem to have some highly placed friends here. But don't get too smart, and be careful. And if you do happen to think of anything else let me know, will you?"

It left me feeling still more uneasy, and still wondering why I had not told him about Angela Caterina.

Miss Harford had taken a table in the front row outside Florian's. In her place, and with her figure and general appearance, I should have been inclined to choose one further back or under the arcade; but a girl who could cause hardened professors to run screaming for shelter was hardly likely to be worried by random passes, not even in the Piazza San Marco. As I crossed the square myself I saw one young hopeful make a good sporting try. So far as I could see she only looked at him enquiringly, but he sheered off as sharply as if an apparently demure little cat had suddenly unsheathed a set of talons. Otherwise she seemed to be quietly enjoying the spectacle. Dark blue slacks, paler blue shirt, white sandals, handbag and linen hat; all perfectly harmless. I said, "I hope you weren't too unkind to him. Some of them are very sensitive."

"That young man?" She smiled at me kindly. "I just told him to go jump in the nearest canal. Quite politely, of course. Did you have a good morning?"

"With Mrs Messina-Silvestro, yes. With Lieutenant Alberti, I'm not so sure. And you?"

"I'm not sure either. I disliked that peculiar way he has of saying 'Yes. . .' As if he's saying it to himself about something he's thinking. But he was still very charming. He said he was distressed about that incident last night, and I said he had no need to be or to waste his very valuable time on it, as I was *quite* satisfied it was just a foolish prank. He said 'Yes. . .' again and then asked what I know about you, and I said, 'Quite a lot.' I told him you are a well-known artist and *very* English, and that you have an odd sense of humour which sometimes makes conversation with you a little curious. And the staff of the Martinelli think very highly of you, which is always a good sign with anybody; and that from what they have told me you have some *very* important friends here in Venice."

My heart warmed to her. She was clever, and she had obviously been doing her best for me. "Did he say anything about the balloon seller?" I asked.

"He did. He asked where and how I had met you. I said I did not consider that was any business of his, but I had no objection to telling him. So I told him about running into you outside the Quattro Fontane, and then he asked had it occurred to me that the balloons might be a sort of marker; so that you should know who you had to pick up."

I said, "Well I'm damned."

"I beg your pardon?" she enquired.

"It's a sort of variation on an idea I had myself," I explained hurriedly. "And what did you say to that?"

"I asked if he imagined I was the sort of person who allows herself to be picked up; which somewhat embarrassed him. Then I said that in any case the first time I noticed this balloon man was at the railroad terminus, when I went there to meet someone off the Munich train, and that you certainly did not try to 'pick me up' then nor on any of the several other occasions afterwards. After that he seemed to be a little at a loss, and I asked him to be good enough to tell you that I should be waiting at Florian's."

"My dear," I said, "you're wonderful; marvellous."

"It is very kind of you to say so, Mr Hedley. But there is no need to get extravagant about it. The point is that the lootenant quite clearly suspects you of something. I feel you should be very, very careful."

"We should both be very careful. Alberti's clever, and he's all set to impress somebody." It was getting time to tell her what had happened to Antonello and warn her about several things on her own account. I went on, "I'd say that so far the top police don't think your balloon man amounts to much because there's something big happening here, or going to happen soon, and they're far more worried about that. It could touch Mrs Messina-Silvestro somehow. But Alberti has an idea that the two things are connected; and so have I. And if that's correct you yourself. . ."

But she was not listening. She was staring across the square instead, and she said, "Wait now. That *girl!* Look!"

I did not need to. Of all the places in Venice where Angela Caterina might have chosen to appear it had to be St Mark's Square at that particular moment; and wearing a wide, brilliantly red hat which was like a beacon. I said, "Hold it, Judith!" but she was off like a cat again. I just had time to catch the nearest waiter, thrust a note at him, and start after her; the pigeons flapping round, a white handbag swinging dangerously, and a blue shirt and slacks pushing through the crowd. The last thing I wanted was a face-to-face stand-up between those two girls. It might seem comic; but so did the balloon man at first.

I heard her call, "Hey, you! I *want* you!" and then Angela Caterina caught sight of her. I saw now that Angela was with a man; and she said something to him and they both turned quickly towards the arch under the clock building. There was the usual crowd here waiting to watch the clock strike, and they hustled through them with the flash of the red hat and Judith barely a dozen paces behind. But then she half fell over a small child, stopped to put him on his feet again, and broke away as I came up to take the full fury of a pair of outraged Italian parents. I got a fist waved under my nose, gathered that we were dangerous imbeciles, said, "*Scusi signore, signora; permesso, urgente*," and escaped somehow just as she got under the arch.

Fortunately the Orologio was packed solid with people and she had now got herself entangled with a florist's porter, a huge basket of flowers on each arm, almost blocking the passage himself, the pair of them trying to fight past each other with his language even more descriptive, and I caught her this time. I said, "For God's sake drop it, will you? You'll start a riot in a minute."

"I will *not* drop it," she snapped back. "I mean to give that girl. . . There it goes," she cried as the red hat bobbed up once more, turning off sharply into a side passage.

She seemed to burrow through the crowd, and short of holding her back by force and starting a really spectacular scene there was no way of stopping her. Rather foolishly I thought that it might not work out so badly after all. Angela Caterina must know this place far better than we did; she could easily give us the slip if she tried, while at the same time I wanted to get a closer look at the man with her if I could. But I should have known nothing would be as simple as that with Miss Harford. When I next caught up with her she said briefly, "Down there. They turned left. *Hurry!* I'm beginning to think you don't want me to catch this girl," she flung back over her shoulder.

"I don't," I admitted, just keeping pace with her, but trying to slow her down slightly, watching the handbag swinging. "I'm terrified. And I thought you said last night was must a silly prank."

"I did. I still do. But I still mean to give that girl a large piece of my mind."

Even now I can't be sure whether they deliberately led us on; but if they did they must have made up their minds what to do very quickly. The fact remains that they just allowed us to keep them in sight. Even in daylight there are parts of Venice which can be very odd; one minute you can be in the thick of a crowd, and then by taking two or three turnings suddenly find youself in a maze of ancient *calli* and passages; some of them barely wide enough to walk abreast. and all silent and deserted. At every corner we caught tantalising glimpses of the white dress and red hat, and the man in light, casual slacks and shirt; and every instinct I had was warning me that the comedy was turning malevolent again. I said, "That's enough, Judith. Let it go."

"I will *not*!" She was totally uncontrollable now. "They went in there. We've *got* them."

It was a little empty square, the only life in it a pair of half-starved cats; and one of the smaller churches with its door wide open, piles of builders' rubble about and no sign of any workmen. There was nobody here to see us, for it was the long midday break, and I should have dragged her away from the place anyhow; but she slipped away from me before I could stop her, and raced across to the doorway. There was nothing else I could do; I went in after her.

Coming from the warmth and sunlight outside it was dim and cold. A high, vaulted cavern with traces of eroded paintings on the walls, a scent of old incense and damp stone, more builders' litter on the floor and steel scaffolding everywhere tapering up into planking and darkness overhead. Even Miss Harford seemed to be slightly put off by the atmosphere. Just for a minute I had the impression of a little girl lost, and there did not appear to be anybody else here. I said coaxingly, "They've dodged us somehow. Come out of it now, Judith."

"They must be here." She shook her head angrily and called, "Where are you?"

The echoes came bouncing back, "You. . . You. . . You. . ." but I heard someone laugh too and caught the glimmer of a white dress flitting across at the far end, vanishing behind what appeared to be a massive tomb. A long creak then, another door opening, widening from a crack to a square of daylight, and the red hat again. Judith started, "There. . ." but at that moment the planking overhead rattled, and we both glanced up. That, or Judith herself, saved my life. She screamed, "Paul!" dragging me aside, and I tripped backwards over a coil of rope just as a ten-foot length of tubular steel came hurtling down like a spear. It struck the pavement six feet away, splitting the stone, sending up a cloud of dust, and filling the place with futher echoes. Then as I got to my feet again there were footsteps hurrying in from the main doorway, a man silhouetted against the light there.

An Italian, very nearly as frightened as we were ourselves, demanding, "What is this; what happened?" He sounded as if he had been hurrying too. "You should not be here; it is forbidden, this church is not open to the public. It is dangerous. *Pericoloso*. You must go. Out!"

"We're going," I told him shortly, and he backed away after us, picking his footing over the rubble on the floor and looking up watchfully at the overhead planking.

Judith was pale, and I was never so thankful to see sunlight myself. She began, "I'm sorry. I shouldn't. . ." but I cut her short. "You weren't to know. We've been lucky. Now we need a drink."

Whoever the man might have been he was turning away in a hurry, and we went in the opposite direction. I had a fair idea of where we were; quite close to the Fenice Theatre square where there is a well-known restaurant, a little enclosure of box trees in pots, a white trellis fence, and a nice public place with people about. Judith was very quiet on the way, even rather meek, but she was getting back to her normal form by the time I planted her down at a table, and said, "Not orange juice, for God's sake." I ordered a Stock for her and a Scotch for myself, put it down almost in one, and then said, "Now listen; I'm going back." She started, "No!" but I went on, "I shan't be long. We're having lunch here, so you can order while I'm away. There's just something I want to check on."

It was only a few minutes, but our man had already been busy. He was there again with another one, apparently the building foreman, and several carabinieri. The foreman was bawling orders, and I got close enough to the doors to see that they had all the working lights on inside, and that the scaffolding was swarming with more carabinieri and workmen. That was all I wanted to see, and I turned back to the Antico Martini and Miss Harford.

She looked at me through the big spectacles, perfectly calm again, faintly owlish—probably the result of the Stock—and I said, "They're searching the place. I thought they might. They won't find anybody of course. Whoever it was must have had plenty of time to get out before the carabinieri arrived. But what's interesting is that they've put a lot of men into it. And the man who turned us out must have been police to call them as quickly as that. And that means that Alberti is still having us tailed. Or just me. I think it's time we started to talk very seriously."

FIVE

We were well through the fish and a flask of white Chianti before I finished. The only thing I had not told her was that I knew who the girl was and where she came from. That, I felt, would only raise fresh complications even if it did not start her off on the warpath again; and I still did not know what to do about Angela Caterina myself. I said, "So there it is," and repeated more or less what I had told Alberti. "I'd say that you know something somebody else wants to know. And it's important. It might help if you could tell me what it is."

She said nothing for quite a long time, thinking about it, but then she shook her head. "I'm sorry, Paul. I wish I could. But. . . It would be breaking a confidence. And it is *very* important."

There was nothing like a ten-foot length of tubular steel for getting her on to Christian names, I thought rather grimly. "For God's sake, don't you see how dangerous it is?" I asked.

"That . . . thing in the church could have been just an accident."

"Antonello could have gone for a midnight swim. But he didn't. That cameraman might have been taking shots of you merely because you're a pretty girl. But he wasn't. You're not really fooling yourself; nor me."

She flushed faintly. "You're getting angry now. I can't really blame you. I should never have let you get yourself caught up. I ought to have frozen you off. I can, you know; and I do usually. But you looked—well; amusing." She stopped again. "I should have to ask someone else. Paul, if we're very, *very* careful will you give me another day or two? It's something which simply must *not* be talked about. But if ever I get my hands on that girl. . ."

"If I get my hands on her you won't have to worry. Look, Judith, if you won't tell me I think you're crazy. But there's nothing to stop me finding out for myself, is there?"

She grinned at me suddenly. "It is a tiny bit Jesuitical perhaps, but I can't really stop you doing that either, can I?"

"It's connected with Mrs Messina-Silvestro."

"Well, that's quite obvious by now. But what I can't understand is why the police should be so concerned. I don't see how it can be their business. Or at least, not yet."

"There is the little matter of Antonello."

"I'd sooner not talk about that. That's too horrible."

The waiter came over then and we broke off. She made a considerable business of deciding whether to have a sweet, cheese or fruit, but when he had gone away again she asked, apparently quite casually, "Do you know anything about Cardinal Giancarlo de' Medici?"

I stared at her blankly. The change of subject was too much for my simple mind. "I've never even heard of him."

"No? He is, or was, a distant ancestor of Mrs Messina-Silvestro. About the middle of the seventeenth century. And even for cardinals in those days he was quite a playboy."

"I see. And that's all you're going to tell me?"

"Was I telling you something?" It was a wonderful act of wide-eyed innocence. "I thought I was just asking."

I said, "I see," again. "So suppose I asked Mrs Messina-Silvestro?"

"About Giancarlo? I imagine you'd get turned out of the house on the spot." She appeared to be concentrating her entire attention on an incredible concoction of ice-cream and glacé fruit, sighing faintly. "I really ought not to eat this. I ought to consider my figure."

"You should. It's worth it. I often find myself considering it too."

There was another of her warm little flushes. "I thought you had other things to think about. And I was wondering whether there might be a portrait of the cardinal in the Ca' Silvestro. Do they have many pictures there?"

I felt that we were just on the verge of more interesting subjects, but I said, "I don't really know. Half a dozen or so in the long corridor; and a few more in the grand salon. But I haven't seen any of the rest of the house."

"I rather think it might pay you to look at them quite closely some time. The pictures, I mean." She sighed again. "That was a beautiful lunch. Thank you, Paul. What are you planning to do this afternoon? After all that wine I really must go back to the pensione; and sleep. I told you I don't drink."

That could be interesting too, I thought; probably exciting. I wondered whether there was the merest hint of invitation there, but she seemed to be concentrating on her coffee now, and I was more worried than I would have cared to admit to her. Another time we hope, I thought, and said, "I couldn't wish for anything better myself. But I've got one or two calls to make."

We took a water-taxi back to Santa Elizabetta; expensive but fast, as the time was getting on now. She was quiet on the way across; quiet and cool when I saw her safely into the Martinelli, but I said, "Wait for me for dinner," and then went straight down to Marco's, picking up a newspaper on the way. It seemed faintly ridiculous, but I sat down and opened the paper, and murmured, "Don't let it look as if we're talking too much, Marco. I'll have a *cappuccino*. Did you contact anybody from the Grand Hotel?"

Marco nodded. All Venetians are born conspirators, as bad as the Romans, and when he brought the coffee he made a big show of wiping off the next table, muttering out of the corner of his mouth. "That's right. There's a Dr Hans Kleber; from Munich. Elderly gentleman. Very quiet. Came about three days ago."

That was all I wanted to know, and I went on reading my paper, finishing the coffee without hurrying over it, and then told him, "If anybody wants to know you can tell them I was asking how I get to San Giorgio Piccolo."

"You take a taxi," he said. "The lagoon boats don't stop there. And it'll cost you. It's a long way."

It was a long way, and it did cost me; and I hoped the visit was going to be worth it. To be quite frank with myself I did not know what I was going to do or say when I got there; especially if I actually found Angela

Caterina. It was just an instinct to feel that I was actively doing something; and I hoped that at least I should not be late for tea. I had an idea that by Mrs Teestock's standards to appear unexpectedly would be a grave social solecism in any case; and to arrive just as they were finishing would make it even worse.

When the boatman at last said, "*Ecco, signore,*" the place surprised me. Very few of the lesser islands in the northern lagoon are particularly attractive, and most are little more than sandbanks, but as we approached this one over the water it looked like something out of a picture-book; small for an island, but large for a private property. Stone landing-steps and a balustrade with urns of flowers on it, a carefully tended stretch of grass, more flower-beds, shrubs and vine pergolas, a low pink-washed Italianate villa-type house, a square four-story tower at one end in a clump of cypress trees. And a group of four people, two women and two men, sitting out on the patio; as I had expected, at afternoon tea.

When I paid off the boatman I looked back over the water. I had not noticed anybody following me on the Lido, and there were only a few sailing-boats and a lagoon ferry out there now; Murano lying in the middle distance, vaguely pink and yellow, Venice gleaming softly in the blue beyond that, but no sign of the spray from another fast launch coming in. It did not matter very much anyhow, I thought, turning up the steps and still wondering how I was to explain myself.

It was a peaceful little scene; a quiet, country house afternoon oddly arrested for a second. Mrs Teestock in the act of pouring tea; d'Espinal pouting at me with a sheaf of ten by eight photographs in his hands; a distinguished, scholarly looking man glancing up at me over the top of another, in the early sixties, thin faced and silver haired, with a neat imperial beard;

and Emilia Pentecost getting up from a long cane chair. She came across the grass to meet me, wearing a cream-coloured dress in soft light wool, expensively simply, saying, "Hallo, Paul. This is quite a surprise."

"Yes. I hope I'm not intruding." It sounded lame. "I was at a loose end; and Mrs Teestock suggested. . ."

"Of course," she said. "We're always delighted to have visitors. Especially you."

"Such a pleasant surprise," Mrs Teestock murmured. "We're so far away we sometimes feel people forget us. Emilia, dear, ask Gabriella to bring another cup and saucer."

D'Espinal was anything but delighted. Amiable again, but the benevolence of the Roman emperor interrupted in important business, gathering the photographs together and laying them face downwards on the cushions of a chair behind; nothing too obvious about it, but putting them well out of the way. "My dear fellow, an unexpected kindness." But there was a momentarily wicked look in his eye. "Doctor Kleber, pray permit me to present Mr Paul Hedley."

He was the only one here to seem faintly amused; and he was certainly the man Judith had been talking to at the Grand Hotel gates last night. He seemed to carry his left arm rather stiffly; not in the most robust of health, I thought, but a decided personality and not one who would come out here merely for small talk. As obviously an expert as Judith herself did not appear to be, and I wondered briefly how well the two of them got on together while he said, "It's a great pleasure, Mr Hedley. I've seen some of your work; though not much, I fear. Not so much as I should like to see."

It was a nice compliment, and I tried a little rather clumsy fishing. "I would have thought it was out of your period, sir. Though I must admit I don't quite know what that is."

D'Espinal was watching me from under half-closed

eyelids, realising that I knew what Doctor Kleber was, but Kleber parried the question neatly. "What is period? Just the very few years which any normally limited person can hope to study in detail."

"You're too modest, Doctor," d'Espinal pronounced heavily. "But how is the portrait coming, Hedley? I really don't envy you your task."

"Milk or lemon, Mr Hedley?" Mrs Teestock asked, and then answered for me. "I hear it's coming along famously. Amelita was scandalised and delighted by the preliminary sketches. She says Mr Hedley is the only man she knows who has ever told her exactly what she is to her face."

Kleber laughed pleasantly. "Then he's a braver man than I am. She's a very old friend of mine, but I've never had the courage to do that."

There was a hint of reaction again from d'Espinal. He moved uneasily in his chair and reached out to take the photographs and slip them into an envelope; a touch of petulance. "You're quite comfortable at the Martinelli I hope, Hedley? And I hope you're respectful to the cat there. He's a very old friend of mine too.'

The doctor glanced quizzically at me. It was obvious that he knew Judith Harford was staying there now, and it seemed more than likely that she had told him something about me. But then Emilia said, "Another boat. Really, we are busy today."

She was looking out over the water, and I turned myself to see a motor-launch cutting in and coming fast judging by the wings of spray it was flinging out; coming too fast. Alberti's men, I wondered? But if they were still tailing me they should have been here long before; and they would never be as blatant as this. So had they discovered something in that church; or had something happened to Judith already? I watched the thing roar in at an insane speed towards the landing-steps and then heel over in a wide curve to throttle down, apparently only just clearing them in time. There was a faint shriek from it, and Emilia said, "Angela, of course. It would be, like that."

"Really," Mrs Teestock murmured. "So *reckless*. Who's driving it, Emilia? Is it that Piretti boy again?" She stopped, looking at me; once again no family troubles before strangers. "Young people, Mr Hedley. If they can't drive cars too fast they drive boats instead. It does so much damage. Can you see who it is, Emilia?"

"I can't." Her tone suggested that she did not want to and did not care. She got up suddenly, catching d'Espinal's eye, and said, "Dr Kleber, I wonder if you'd like to come up to the studio? Will you excuse us, Paul?"

I watched the girl scrambling out. She seemed to have caught a good deal of the spray, for her dress was soaked, clinging to her figure. It looked as if she had very little if anything on underneath, but she was laughing, and she waved and called out something as the boat heeled again and roared away. Mrs Teestock made disapproving noises as she turned and started to run across the grass towards us; but then she caught sight of me and stopped dead. She was surprised and frightened, yet it was not quite the sort of sheer panic I expected. It was more the uneasiness of a child caught out in a piece of mischief, and she even managed to work up a small, half-placatory smile, but Mrs Teestock demanded, "What on earth have you been doing?"

She barely glanced at the older woman. "I got wet."

"So it appears," Mrs Teestock snapped. "Go and change at once. You look indecent." But at that moment a telephone started ringing in the house, and she said, "Oh dear. Do please excuse me, Mr Hedley. Go and change, Angela."

Emilia Pentecost, Dr Kleber and d'Espinal had already gone, and I waited until Mrs Teestock hurried in through the French windows and then said softly, "Not yet. I like you like that, my dear. We're going to talk while we've got the chance. Anywhere you like; but not here. And if you don't talk to me you'll talk to the police."

"The police?" She was still watching me, working something out, and she nodded. She called, "All right, Aunt Teestock; but I'm going to show Mr Hedley round," and glanced at me over her shoulder, saying, "This way, then. I've got a very special place."

Along under the vine pergola, under an archway, and round the side of the building we were in a well-kept garden where there was a middle-aged Italian hoeing peacefully among the plants, and she recited, "As you see, this is our garden. We are very proud of it. The person you see not working very hard there is Pietro. Pietro is our man about the house, and when he is not working very hard at anything else he drives our boat for us; when he puts on a blue jacket and white cap, which is the correct thing to do in Venice. Pietro adores Mrs Teestock. So do they all; they all adore Mrs Teestock. Mrs Pietro is our cook, and Gabriella is our maid, and there are several sisters and cousins who appear from time to time; which is an old Italian custom. The Pietros have a flat on the middle floors of the tower which you see on our right. Miss Emilia Pentecost has her studio on the top floor of the same tower, where she does some very interesting things. I call it the Tower of the Mysteries, and you would be very interested. . ."

"I'm not," I cut in. "I'm more interested in your little bit of fun in that church this morning. Which of us were you aiming to kill? Judith Harford or me?"

She stopped dead again. "Kill? What d'you mean?"

I told her, as briefly and brutally as possible, and

this time she was badly frightened. She said shrilly, "That's not true. I don't believe it. Toni said it was just going to be a joke. He was just going to drop some mess on you. Dust and plaster and stuff."

"He dropped a ten-foot length of steel; and it came down end on. And the police saw it happen. They were searching the place when I left." It was clear enough that she had been out of the church before the tube dropped, but there was no harm in stretching the truth a bit, I thought. "I'd say your humorous friend is probably trying to answer some very pointed questions by now." Then I noticed the gardener, Pietro, watching us with interest, and I said, "Get on then. Let's get to this particular place of yours."

"What are you going to do?" she asked.

She led the way across the garden and through a belt of shrubbery out on to a sudden, surprising little beach. A half moon of sand screened by tall tamarisk scrub, a big sun-shade and seats, a bathing-chalet and boat-house, a long plank jetty and a diving-raft floating offshore.

"All my very own," she said. "It's pretty, isn't it? Harry set it up just for me. Nobody ever comes here; so what are you going to do?" She kicked off her sandals, digging her toes into the warm sand, looking at me out of the corners of her eyes with her head tilted slightly sideways. "You're lying, you know. Toni said to wait for him outside, so I waited, and then he came out and we went to Harry's Bar. So the police can't really be asking him questions, can they?"

"Just as you like," I said. "I'll get them over here tonight. Then they can ask you."

"You'll be a fool if you do. If I started talking to the police I could blow this place sky-high; and the Ca' Silvestro. Not that somebody else doesn't mean. . ." She stopped and giggled. "I could blow the Messina hag with it; and Aunt Teestock and Harry and Emilia

Pentecost here. I know what they're doing, you see. I know what they've been doing for the last two years, and I know what they're trying to do now. God, I'd love to see that bitch sweating it in an Italian prison. Signorina Emilia wouldn't be so cool then. Of course, I wouldn't like it so much for. . ."

She checked herself, and I stared at her. I had been starting to think that she was slightly schizophrenic, but I realised suddenly that she was in love with that great fat buffoon; jealous of Emilia Pentecost and incredibly naïve with it. I could almost have felt sorry for her, but she went on petulantly, "Damn this dress. It's uncomfortable."

It was quite obvious what was coming next, and I sat down on one of the seats while she peeled it over her head. As I had suspected she was naked underneath it, but she appeared to be disappointed by my lack of interest. "Don't you think it's nice?"

"It's certainly not bad. What happened to your red hat?"

"It blew away in the boat." She was a sulky little girl now, angry because she had lost something she treasured. "I only got it yesterday."

"That's a pity. You ought to have it on now; just the hat. It would add to the general effect. Who's the Piretti boy?"

"Oh God," she asked, "must we talk about him? We could go into the chalet," she suggested. "I might tell you what they're all doing."

"We could; and you might," I agreed. "But I know already." Again not strictly true, or not yet, but I did not need any help from little Angela to find out. "Tell me what you know about a man named Antonello instead."

"That jerk?" she shrugged, raising her breasts deliberately. "He just sells stuff."

"I noticed them." I told her mildly. "There's no

need to wave them in front of my eyes. And there's a correction. Antonello *did* sell stuff. Pot, for instance. He was murdered the other night. I've got a feeling that you're playing with boys and girls far away out of your class, Angela Caterina."

There was no way of telling whether I was getting home to her, nor whether she really knew what had happened to Antonello. She certainly did not seem to care. She was standing with one hand on her hip, the other fingering a tendril of hair hanging down over her shoulder, one knee thrust forward, her head still tilted slightly. It looked as if she picked up the pose from one of the girlie magazines and practised it. She asked, "Is there anything wrong with you?" and then, with one of her lightning changes of subject, "I must say I'm starting to get very bored with some of them."

"You should be careful they don't get bored with you. Like they did with Antonello."

"They won't do that; they can't." She shook her head. "They need me. I put them on to it in the first place you see. I could tell you too. I could tell you what the boys are planning if you're nice to me."

"I've told you, my dear, I already know. I'm going to be very nice to you anyway," I promised. "You're irresistible. I always fall for a pretty girl. But there's only one thing before we have fun. I want your boys to lay off Judith Harford and me. I don't much care what they're doing, but just one more little joke like today and they'll have trouble. So will you. Is that understood?" She nodded, and I got up slowly from the seat. "We'll understand each other better still in a minute. Did you say the chalet?"

"Yes please," she whispered. "Be quick."

"It won't be long," I said, picking her up with one arm under her knees and the other round her waist. "You've got me impatient too. Just close your eyes and relax." She really did need a psychiatrist, I thought briefly, for she made it surprisingly easy, acting out some sort of private fantasy. She went limp in my arms, with her eyes closed obediently, and it was only half a dozen paces to the jetty and a few more along the planking to the deep water. Just as we got to the end she realised suddenly what was going to happen to her and started to claw at me, but it was too late then. She went in and down almost before she had time to shriek; and at the same time I saw Emilia emerge from the path through the tamarisks.

Angela came up coughing, spitting out a breathless stream of gutter Italian. For a minute it looked as if she was going to come back fighting at the jetty, but I said, "It's all very silly; let's call it a day, my dear," and she rolled over in the water like a fish and swam strongly out to the diving-raft. Emilia had watched the whole ridiculous scene dispassionately, but when I got back up the beach to her I felt some form of apology was called for. "I'm sorry about that. It was rather schoolboyish."

"I suppose it was." She watched Angela Caterina expressionlessly, now climbing on to the raft, balancing there with her feet braced well apart, gleaming wetly in the sunlight and raising her hands to push her hair back. "It was quite pleasantly decisive though. Were you seriously considering drowning her?"

The comedy turning vicious again, I thought uneasily. "Not really. I thought she might like that better than being told not to be a little fool."

"She will, of course." Emilia seemed to be faintly regretful. "It's a pity. Somebody will have to do it sooner or later. But what I really came to tell you, Paul, is that Dr Kleber is just going back in our boat if you care to go with him. It will save you calling a taxi out. They're so wickedly expensive these days."

* * *

Dr Kleber was friendly but uncommunicative although we had plenty of time to talk during the first part of the trip, since Pietro appeared to be one of the slower and more sedate drivers. As carefully as possible I tried to find out how long the doctor had been friendly with Mrs Messina-Silvestro, but gathered very little except that he had known the family through her brother, as young men before and during the war years. We talked about the rescue work in Venice, which apparently he considered was now too slow and too late, and then he switched the subject to the other lagoon islands as we cruised past them. There was a pretty little legend about San Francesco del Deserta, he said; where St Francis of Assisi was supposed to have once landed during a storm and planted his stick in the sand; which immediately grew into a blossoming tree filled with birds singing to the Saint while he took shelter beneath it.

He was just pointing out the distant building of the monastery there, gleaming in the sunlight behind us, when I caught sight of the other boat closing up on us, almost in our wake. I was still listening to the doctor, and it did not seem to be particularly threatening except that it was bigger and heavier than ours, and that its flared bows were built for power and speed. But then, as I watched, it accelerated and they lifted higher out of the water. I know nothing about manoeuvring speed-boats, but even I could see that it would be alongside within a minute, at least swamping us in its wash. It seemed to be hurtling down on us like a shark, and both Kleber and I called out to Pietro. He too turned in his seat to look back, and cursed suddenly.

He yelled, "Bloody madmen!" and took instant evasive action, ramming at the throttle and swinging off in a tight curve. Our boat seemed literally to leap out of the water. Kleber crashed into me as we heeled, and I barely saved him from going in himself. Then we clung on to everything we could hold, sprawling on the floor-boards, already half awash and with sheets of spray hissing past. Braced in his seat, clinging to the wheel and still cursing, Pietro was pulling round in a wide circle at top speed, trying to get as far as possible behind the other boat to meet the wash nose on. I caught a glimpse of it passing, so fast that it was half hydroplaning, and heard its motors roaring though now mercifully some distance off, and then we hit the first wave and bounced.

As waves go it was probably not much, but it looked and felt like a rolling wall of green glass in front of us. We struck it with a shuddering jar which seemed to travel all the way up one's spine, and then hung visibly in the air before hitting the next. Pietro yelled to keep still, screaming prayers and curses in the same breath, and at one moment I thought our hull had split under the repeated crashes; our motor spluttered and died, and I heard Dr Kleber making some decidedly unacademic remarks in German while we wallowed and rolled. But then miraculously it caught again, and Pietro somehow pulled us round once more, half waterlogged but now merely swooping sickeningly over the ridges instead of bumping and skidding from one to the next. He released the wheel just long enough to raise both fists and shake them at the other boat, weeping with fury and screaming, "Holy Mother of Jesus, if ever I get these big hands on you bastards. . ."

As I got to my feet and helped Kleber up it was lying idly about a quarter mile away, its engines still muttering, and for a moment I thought it was coming back for another try; but there was a ferry in sight now and it sheered off suddenly, lifting up in a fresh cloud of spray and heading away towards Murano. "But why?" Pietro demanded helplessly. "Why me and my boat? What have I done? That wicked bitch daughter of a Chioggia whore. . . One day. . ."

He made an expressive, murderous little wringing movement with his hands, and I asked, "Who were they? Did you see them? And what in hell were they trying to do, anyway? If they'd hit us they'd have smashed themselves."

Pietro seemed to think I was simple-minded. "I did not see them; I did not have time. You notice I was busy, eh? But I know. They were trying to turn us over." The big hands came into play again. "Like that; in their wash. It is easily done. And now we get out of this quick."

"Two men, both quite young," Kleber murmured quietly as we got under way again, very much faster now. "It was the same boat which brought the young lady to San Giorgio this afternoon, was it not?"

"It appeared to be. But they all look very much alike."

"Meaning we could not identify it again?" He looked at me thoughtfully. "That is true of course. I certainly could not. Would you say it was simply an insane practical joke?"

"We both know it was a great deal more than that. The point is, do we report it to the police?"

"If we cannot identify the boat what is the use? If you wish to do so I have no right to stop you of course. But for the next day or two the last thing I want is to have the Italian police pestering me." He corrected himself quickly. "Or at any other time for that matter."

He was still being uncommunicative, and neither of us said much more. But I thought that we were all taking crazy risks now, merely for the sake of trying to cover up whatever it was that somebody had discovered in the Ca' Silvestro.

SIX

When I got back to the Martinelli they told me that Signorina Harford had gone out, and I passed a fresh half-hour of uneasiness while I showered and changed; but when I went down to the terrace she was sitting there with the cat, both of them gazing rather distastefully at a glass of Campari soda. Otherwise the scene was unchanged in the interlude before dinner; the priest and the French gentleman talking quietly together, the French gentleman's wife industriously writing postcards, the plump and placid lady still knitting. Judith said, "I was just beginning to get a *very* little bored. And I can't think why I asked for this stuff. It tastes quite revolting."

"It is," I agreed. "Did you have a pleasant afternoon?"

"I slept very peacefully. Did you? Have a nice afternoon I mean?"

"It was active. Interesting; even informative in a

negative sort of way." Graziella came out as breathlessly as ever, and I asked her for a large Scotch. That was always worth while, if only for the thrill it gave the child; she seemed to consider that she was serving something really exciting and wicked. I asked, "Did Lieutenant Alberti call?"

"If he did nobody's told me. Were you expecting him to?"

"I thought he might after this morning. But I'm not quite sure what to expect any more. And I'm not sure whether calling or not calling is the more sinister."

Judith seemed to be studying me with a rather more than usual interest. "Did you know that you have a very distinct scratch on your face?"

"I noticed it for the first time a few minutes ago. I must have caught myself against something. As I said, I had an active afternoon. Among other things I went to look for your friend in the red hat."

Judith stared at me for a second and then almost miaowed. "So you did know her! I suspected that, Paul Hedley. Your face when you caught sight of her at Florian's this morning. The way you were very careful not to catch up with her. I'm beginning to feel that you are very, *very* devious, and I've a right to an explanation. And if the lootenant does not call us, we call him. Right now."

I said, "I'm afraid we can't."

The green sparks were starting to flash behind her spectacles again. "And why ever not?"

"It might get awkward for several people; including Mrs Messina-Silvestro. As you say, you're entitled to an explanation. Her name is Angela Caterina, and she is the ward or adoptee of Sir Harcourt d'Espinal and or Mrs Teestock on an island called San Giorgio Piccolo. You probably know d'Espinal?"

But Miss Harford was still not giving too much away either. "I know of him." She asked, "You went to San

Giorgio this afternoon?"

"And I met Dr Hans Kleber, of Munich." I waited for her, but she did not say anything, and I went on, "He's a very nice man and I wouldn't like anything to happen to him. But we'll come to Dr Kleber later. Let's keep to Angela Caterina. She might be a psychiatric case, but I don't think she is. I'd say she's bored, spoiled, living in a fantasy world of her own because she doesn't have anything else to do, and playing for kicks."

"I'll say she is. It was some kick in that church this morning."

"She swears she doesn't know anything about that. And I'm inclined to believe her."

There was a touch of acid in Judith's voice; she looked rather pointedly at the scratch on my face. "You seem to have enjoyed quite a heart to heart talk."

"It was hardly that. I warned her in effect that she was getting into something out of her depth; and I told her to advise her boyfriends to lay off you and me. Apparently I should have included Dr Kleber as well."

"What's happened to Hans, then?" Judith asked sharply.

"Nothing much; so far. He should be safely back at the Grand Hotel by now. I said we'd come to him in a minute. I told Angela Caterina that if we had even the hint of any more trouble I should get straight on to the police. And she said if I did she could talk to them too."

"About what?"

"That's rather the point of the whole thing, isn't it? I wouldn't be able to guess myself if it weren't for another character involved. A Miss Emilia Pentecost. Do you know her too?"

Judith shook her head. "I don't."

"Emilia recommended me to paint this portrait of Mrs Messina-Silvestro, though I'm not quite clear why;

or not yet. She's close to d'Espinal; probably his mistress, certainly his business associate. And d'Espinal makes a profession of tracing lost works of art. Judging by their life-style he also makes a good thing out of it."

"At today's values he would," Judith said. "If he's successfull."

"He appears to be extraordinarily successful; with Emilia Pentecost's help. Emilia's a painter too; in several ways a very remarkable painter. I knew her fairly well; some years ago in Paris. We were both having a bad time in different ways. I hadn't yet started to persuade the right people to say I was good; she was having a miserable love-affair. And she was also just beginning to realise that if she lived to be a hundred she would never make a genuinely creative artist. In the end I took off to tramp down to the Riviera, and while I was there my luck took a spectacular turn for the better. So it was another year or so before I was back around the Boul' Mich' again; when I heard that a wealthy relative had appeared from somewhere and whisked Emilia away."

"How very sad." Judith's voice was sweetly sympathetic. "And is this . . . a little bit of unfinished business?"

"It is not. I'm merely telling you because it may have a distinct bearing on what is happening now; and on what Angela Caterina might talk about. Emilia was an incredibly skilful copyist. In those days you could just about make a living out of selling quite honest copies of famous pictures. Emilia worked on several, but she had one particular speciality; I remember her once telling me that the simpering bitch was quietly driving her mad. That was La Gioconda; Leonardo da Vinci's Mona Lisa in the Louvre."

Nice little Judith suddenly became the terror of hardened old professors again. "I know who painted La Gioconda, and where it is, thank you," she said tartly. It was a good enough obvious reaction to cover another one less obvious, I thought. She asked, "So what are you suggesting?"

"Simply that if d'Espinal can't trace a lost work of art they manufacture it."

"I see," she murmured. "Yes, indeed I see that it might be *very* awkward if this unpleasant little creature Angela Caterina were to talk about anything like that. And as Mis Pentecost is an old friend of yours you're naturally reluctant. . ."

"Let's say I'm hesitating," I cut in sharply. "But only so long as nothing else happens. If it does the police will have to come in; and it certainly will be awkward for everybody concerned. You mentioned today's values yourself. At those prices, and if I'm right, d'Espinal and Emilia Pentecost must be practising fraud on a colossal scale. If you call it fraud."

I could have sworn somehow that she was slightly relieved. I was getting close to the mark, but I had not quite got it yet. She asked, "And what do you call it? What is your moral attitude?"

"I'm not sure that I have one. I'm inclined to feel that if people are prepared to pay thousands of pounds a square inch for more or less nicely arranged paint, just so long as it's under a particular name, they deserve all they get. The whole business has become an absurdly inflated racket. Most of these things only get locked away in strong rooms anyhow. Very few people ever see them."

"That is a very, *very* reprehensible point of view,." she said severely.

"Yes, isn't it. But with Mrs Messina-Silvestro involved there's another angle. She's spending a fortune on shoring up and restoring the Ca' Silvestro; and so far as I can make out she's given as much more away for other work. I rather think that's why d'Espinal, Emilia Pentecost, Mrs Teestock and Dr

Kleber are all in it with her. But I can't see a man of Kleber's stature lending himself to forgery."

"Indeed you can't. Nor myself, I hope."

"So there has to be something bigger still behind it all. Something which must run to hundreds of thousands, or even millions; dollars or pounds. And little Angela claims she can blow that wide open too if she tries. So what do *we* do?"

"I really think that it's getting time rather to decide what to do to little Angela," Judith murmured. "Not that I'm suggesting anything, of course." She paused to dip her forefinger experimentally in the Campari and offer it to the cat. He sneezed at her rudely and stalked away, and she said, "Oh dear, I've offended him now. One really can't blame him. You're making some very clever guesses, Paul. Or was it Hans Kleber? You said you met him this afternoon. Did he tell you anything?"

"I'm making some very clever guesses. Dr Kleber was as reticent as you are. All he did say what that the last thing he wants is to be pestered by the police."

I told her about afternoon tea on San Giorgio and the ride back with Kleber. When I went on about the boat incident she stared at me without moving or speaking until I finished, and then said, "Well, I don't know. I simply do not know. This is getting very serious, Paul." As a classic understatement it was almost British I thought, but she asked, "Why? What were they trying to do?"

"They meant to swamp us or turn us over. They were after Kleber. They'd have picked him up and left Pietro and me. They might have done more than just leave us."

"Yes. I. . ." She made one of her little hand gestures. Not funny this time; rather helpless and angry. "But how could they know that Hans was going to be there?"

"Isn't it obvious? Dr Kleber knows his social

manners. He wouldn't dream of dropping in at San Giorgio without an invitation like I did. Angela Caterina knew he was going to be there and told them. So they brought her back after a jolly morning in Venice, and then just lay off out of sight and waited. And that had the extra advantage of leaving her in the clear again. She wouldn't have to know what they were going to do."

"Damn Angela Caterina," Judith said. "And I may say, Paul Hedley, that *you* seem to be going away out to protect her all you can. I shall soon start to take a real dislike to that girl." She stopped suddenly. "No, Paul; I'm sorry. If I go on like this I shall soon have you taking a dislike to me. I wouldn't want that. And I'm sorry that if Hans Kleber didn't see fit to tell you anything I can't either. It really is big. Perhaps bigger than even you think."

"And you can't talk because Kleber actually called you in?" I asked. "For your expert opinion?" That really did seem to surprise her, and I said, "Don't let it worry you. I'm quite enjoying working it out for myself."

"You are getting angry," she said sadly. "I'm in a very invidious position, Paul."

"So that makes all of us. But it still leaves the sixty-four thousand dollar question. Where do we go from here?"

She looked at me speculatively. "It rather seems to me that you've already gone some distance. And we're agreed that none of us wants the police in. So far as I can see that only leaves one alternative."

"There is another. You and Kleber could get out of Venice; fast." She did not even stop to think about it; she shook her head, and for some reason I felt absurdly relieved. I said, "It's obstinate, my dear; but it suits me. So long as you realise that we're asking for trouble."

* * *

Dinner was coming up then, but Judith went off to make a quick call to Kleber; raising one eyebrow slightly when I hinted that it might be just as well to be careful about what she said. She appeared to think that I was underrating her, but I had a strong feeling that if Alberti was only half as worried and ambitious as I took him to be he would have a tap on that telephone by now. I ordered another Scotch, mainly for the sake of watching little Graziella's delighted horror and then Judith's faint disapproval when she came back; the other eyebrow just as slightly raised this time. It was amazing how she could use whichever one she pleased.

She said, "He's quite all right. He was even rather rude when I told him that he ought to stay in tonight in case he's taken a chill from the wetting. He said that there was no need to go out of my way to remind him of his own daughter; and he was planning to in any case. There's a Mozart concert in the hotel, and he intends to sit in on it. That should be safe enough." She paused. "He also said that you saved him from being flung out of that boat this afternoon; at quite some risk to yourself."

"Did I?" I was pleasantly surprised. "I didn't notice."

In fact I hadn't. Those few minutes had been too chaotic to notice anything very much except water, but the improved approval was gratifying. She said, "He seems to have taken quite a liking to you. He suggests we have lunch together tomorrow. And Sir Harcourt d'Espinal called him a few minutes ago," she added. "He was very angry and alarmed, but Hans told him he was satisfied that it was just stupid young men fooling about." She paused. "Sir Harcourt's going to call you too."

I said, "Damn that. That might be awkward." I

explained quickly, "If Lieutenant Alberti's playing this the way I think he is he's got a tap on that telephone by now. And if d'Espinal starts talking about funny business with boats and happens to mention names it could lead the lieutenant straight on to Dr Kleber."

"Oh dear," she murmured. "Yes; I see. So what?"

"So I'm going out. I want you to take the call. Say what you like, but stall him. Don't let him talk." She looked as if she was about to argue, the terror of the professors again, but I went on, "There might be another call; from a friend of mine named Manny Levin. Just tell him I'll call him back."

"And what else would you like me to do?" she enquired. "And what about dinner? And where are you going?"

"I'd as soon you sat here safely with the cat all night, and I'm sorry about dinner. So you can apologise to the Martinellis for me too. Tell them I've had to go to Mrs Messina-Silvestro's; they'll understand that. I'm going to Harry's Bar; I've heard it mentioned once or twice." But I thought that at this point it would be just as well not to say any more about Angela Caterina. "It's one of the very smart spots, and I might pick up a lead there. If I don't I shall go on to a place called Benito's in the Calle della Fava. After that I shall catch the last ferry which gets back here about twelve, if you care to wait up for me."

"Paul Hedley . . ." she started, but then stopped. The priest, the placid lady and the French gentleman all seemed to be watching us with great interest, and she said meekly, "Very well then." Far too meekly. I should have been warned.

I went round to Marco's first. At this time of the evening the crowds were thinning out, drifting back from the bathing-beaches to their hotels or across to Venice, but so far as I could see there was still no sign of anybody tailing me. Marco received me with a touch of reserve. I had a feeling that he was fascinated, but starting to wish I would take my custom somewhere else; and when I asked if there had been any enquiries that afternoon he repeated, "Enquiries? My God, all of Venice is enquiring for you," He shrugged. "Well, not all of Venice; but three."

He counted them off on his fingers. "First, a cop. Plain-clothes. But I know them all, and the smell they carry around with them; like cold coffee. Next, a young signorina."

"Very pretty?" I asked. "White dress and red hat?"

He nodded and sketched a shape with both hands. "And what beautiful eyes. *Mama mia*, if that one were looking for me I would not hide myself."

"You might," I said. "You might run screaming. And who was the last one?"

This time he seemed to suggest that I was getting myself into some really undesirable company. "A priest."

The policeman I had expected; Angela Caterina did not surprise me much; but the priest was really startling. "For God's sake," I said, "what sort of priest?"

Marco shrugged again. "You know priests. When you've seen one you've seen them all. They come fat or lean and pale or pink. This one was of the middle sort. He asked could I tell him where Signor Hedley had departed for, and I told him Signor Hedley had departed for Isola San Giorgio Piccolo, and he then ordered a *cappuccino* and sat here communing with himself. Which is also a way priests have, and more than either of the others did. The signorina merely asked if you had been seen here since lunch, and then ran off quickly towards the boats, and the cop said, 'Thank God, so I can have a quiet afternoon.' Except when they are making trouble cops are always lazy bastards."

"But what sort of priest?" I insisted. "Italian? German? English?"

"How can one tell? He spoke good Italian." Marco eyed me rather sourly. "*Interessante*, eh? Maybe I should keep a book to write their names down? Or do you want to leave any more messages?"

"Yes," I said. "If anybody asks tonight tell them I've gone across to Harry's Bar. And give yourself an Old Roman for me when you feel you need it."

It was just getting dusk, opalescent blue again, and the waterfront lamps coming up like big pinkish pearls, when I went over. At this slack hour of the evening the ferry was half empty, and there was space enough to look around and work out how Antonello, the balloon seller, had been sent overboard. It seemed all too easy from the sides towards the stern, with the very few passengers on the last crossing upstairs in the bar, and the captain and crew in the natural course of events looking out the way the boat was travelling. All over and out of sight in a few seconds; and if anybody had chanced to come down and catch a glimpse of what looked like a struggle his assailants—certainly two and probably more—could have just as easily pulled him back and then explained that the man was drunk and they had actually saved him from going over. There had been practically no risk to it. It was doubtful whether even Antonello himself had ever really known what was happening to him.

As Alberti had said coldly, he was no great loss to anybody; his murder was police business, not mine. But what came home to me most forcibly, I think for the first time on that particular twenty minutes crossing, was the apparently random way these people moved. It struck me suddenly that they were reckless amateurs; and that really did frighten me. You know that professionals will not take unnecessary risks, you at least have a chance of guessing what they might do next; but amateurs are always dangerously incalculable. There was no doubt that they had an ultimate objective, and none that it was aimed at something of immense value discovered at the Ca' Silvestro in the course of the reconstruction work; and that something, somewhere, had gone wrong. So now they were blundering about wildly; taking quick, unpredictable chances.

There was also no doubt that Hans Kleber and Judith had been called in to evaluate the Ca' Silvestro discovery; or more probably that d'Espinal had called in Kleber, and that he in turn had brought in Judith. But that still did not explain where Emilia Pentecost and her skills as a copyist came into it; for if there was one thing absolutely certain, it was that a man of Kleber's reputation and integrity would never lend himself to anything which had the slightest hint of forgery. Neither did it explain Alberti's interest and anxiety, nor the carabinieri outside the Silvestro house and the curious atmosphere inside. That could only mean that somewhere there was a separate threat to some other person; almost certainly Mrs Messina-Silvestro herself. Or could this threat and the discovery of an unknown work of art be connected somehow?

Finally none of it explained the sudden appearance of a priest in the party. That seemed to be completely inexplicable. But was he the priest who was staying at the Martinelli, and if so was he also connected with Judith and Kleber? He seemed to keep strictly to himself; pleasant enough, though with no more than a nod and a smile when we happened to meet, and so far apparently she had not shown the slightest sign of interest in him. The priest worred me. He seemed to be another random element, but one could never tell with Judith; she obviously still considered herself bound by some sort of professional arrangement with Kleber. But tomorrow, I thought, as the boat nudged into the landing-stage at San Zaccaria, when we had lunch together, one of them had to talk.

Harry's Bar is one of the fashion spots of Venice. It lies rather secretively in the Calle Vallaresso just behind the San Marco airways and motor-boat terminal, and it is a curious mixture of nineteenth-century Mid-Western saloon and modern, expensive Italian restaurant; swing doors to the street, a boarded floor, dark woodwork and a long bar with high stools, and at the same time tables with pink tablecloths, napkins and candles. Consequently it attracts two entirely different types of clientele; tourists who are edged to the tables by the waiters and who come once only for the sake of saying they have been here, something to talk about back at home, and a distinctive type of smart Venetian and cosmopolitan European at the bar. One set watching, and the other providing the show.

It was a natural haunt for Angela Caterina and her curious playmates, but I would never have expected to find anybody from the Ca' Silvestro in the crush at the bar. So I was all the more surprised to see Celia van Druyten there.

She appeared to be talking to a man who struck me as being vaguely familiar, although it was difficult to place him in that light and the smoky atmosphere, and just as difficult to work through to get closer to them. Broken bubbles of conversation and a surrealist effect again. A black velvet Renaissance hat and a sweeping feather, an elderly face painted like a fretful childish doll, a check flannel shirt open to the navel and a vast red beard declaiming, "I spit me at the committee of the Biennale"; a whispy little creature with lank silver hair and smudged eyes asking, "Do I *know* you?" and a plaintive American voice enquiring, "You wanna get by the bar? So I wanna get *out*." But I was near enough to be sure then. It was the cameraman who had been taking shots of Judith in the carrozza on the Viale Elizabetta the other day.

So far neither of them had seen me. I had wedged myself in so that I was back to back with Celia, and the man was looking down thoughtfully at his drink; but now one of the barmen condescended to notice my existence for the first time, and I had to order. I barely more than shaped "Bourbon on the rocks" with my lips and then half turned my head to try to hear what they were saying. I just caught, ". . . searched the house, of course. The police seem to be starting to think it's a hoax. They say none of the people they would expect to be responsible are in Venice." He asked something which I could not catch, and she said, "I think it's hateful. . . Saturday. . ."

I was doing well, although again I missed what the man answered. The noise all round seemed to be rising and falling in waves, the barman was rattling a cocktail shaker, and the bearded clown a few feet away was still announcing what he would do to the Biennale committee; I heard Celia say, "Five million dollars should be enough. . ." But at that moment he appeared to notice a long-lost friend approaching and bellowed, "André, *amico*," flung out his arms, lurched off his stool to embrace him, and sent a shock-wave all along the bar. It was unavoidable. The cameraman looked up over Celia's shoulder, she herself turned round saying acidly, "Pardon me," and recognition was all round and instantaneous.

There was a little frozen pause, and then she said, "Why, Mr Hedley, how surprising to see you here. And how nice," she added as an afterthought, while the cameraman stared at me briefly. An unpleasant stare;

as unpleasant as that voice on the telephone.

I was prepared to be just as unpleasant myself. I wanted to get him to say something clearly, to be sure, and I moved suddenly to get at him. But he was behind Celia, already backing away, and at the same time we were hemmed in by a fresh party surging in front of him. In another second he had gone; short of fighting my way out there was nothing I could do, and Celia was watching me; not too pleasant herself. She was worried. She said, "Why, you look quite angry. It is a crush, isn't it? Have you been here long?"

"Not long. Just long enough to get a drink and nearly have it knocked out of my hand." She made sympathetic noises, and I said, "Your friend seems to have left very quickly."

"My friend?" She was obviously calculating how much to tell me, but far too clever to say she did not know him. She raised one shoulder. "Hardly that." The voice was light and cool again; indifferent. "He's some sort of television person. Apparently he's making a film about private art collections in Venice and wants permission to come and take pictures in the Ca' Silvestro. It's impossible, of course. Mrs Messina-S. just wouldn't dream of it."

"It seems hard luck on him. Is there anything very important there?"

"There aren't any Titians if that's what you mean. But some quite good things otherwise."

She did not seem to be very interested, but I asked, "Is he connected with the other company? Somebody was telling me there's quite a big outfit here; making a film about Venice in Crisis."

"I've no idea." Even less interested. "I wouldn't think so. I had the impression that he's simply a sort of free-lance." She was looking around the bar. "I must go. I really came to meet some other friends, coming in from Philadelphia. But it seems they haven't arrived."

There was a brief, cool smile. "And I'm afraid Mrs Messina-S. wouldn't approve of my being here."

I watched her slip away neatly through the crowd, one more brief smile before she finally vanished, and I thought it wasn't much but it was something; if only one knew what. It was then nine-fifteen, and I wondered if the chance of picking up anything else, however small, was worth enduring this place for much longer before going on to look for Carson. I asked the barman, "Do the lady and gentleman come here very often?"

It was a silly question to ask a well-trained man, and I got a silly answer. He gave me a wall-faced stare, murmured that one saw so many ladies and gentlemen, and I told him to forget it. Nevertheless there was an unmistakably speculative look in his eye, and I ordered another Bourbon, slipped in a tip respectable enough even by Harry's Bar standards and said, "I'm looking for Toni Piretti. I've got a message for him; from Isola San Giorgio Piccolo. But I don't know him. Is he in here tonight?"

The look turned from speculative to curious and then slightly puzzled. He did not say anything, but moved away, and I was left nursing my Bourbon and watching the ice melt, thinking that this would have to be the last here; apart from wasting time the evening was getting to be expensive, and Mr Barbarossa was beginning to irritate me seriously. His party had been swollen by two more characters, one wearing what appeared to be a red velvet Victorian tablecloth and carrying a fan made of aspidistra leaves, the other in the brown habit and rope girdle of a Franciscan friar with its face and hands made up in shades of green. From Barbarossa's bellows of delight I gathered it was intended to be an El Greco happening to be presented at the Biennale, and the tourists were more than getting their money's worth, but to me it looked distinctly odd. Whether it was the Bourbon or the atmosphere I had a feeling that things were turning unreal again, and I was starting to get susperstitious about that. After the comedy comes the malice, I thought. It was time to go and find something solid; like Carson.

But before I could get out there was another one suddenly beside me, leaning against the bar. Not more than twenty, if that, slightly built but athletic, and undeniably handsome if you like the dark look, an open-necked shirt and casual, Roman-cut slacks and jacket. Expensive, and undoubtedly the perfect type of one of Angela Caterina's little playboys. He was Italian, but he spoke a sort of phony American. "Hi, there. Are you the guy who's asking for Toni Piretti?"

"I was," I said shortly. "But I'm leaving."

"Say now," he protested, "don't be like that. Be my guest." He nodded to the barman, said, "Same again for this gentleman, Sammy," and went on, "Toni's not here right now. But I guess I could find him for you if it's important."

"I don't accept drinks from strange men," I told him. "I don't mean to stay long enough to buy one back. And it's not."

He grinned at me amiably. "Regard it as my pleasure. You sure must want Toni bad if you're prepared to sit out this circus all by yourself. I guess some of the other guys will know where he is. I'll ask around for you."

People seemed to be developing a tendency to appear and disappear. Scarcely had that one vanished behind Barbarossa and his nightmarish green friar before another apparition materialised beside them. A woman this time, almost startlingly tall from the effect of the hair dressed on top of her head in a sort of coronet style and a long purple and dull gold caftan; pale make-up and green eye-shadow, elongated black-rimmed eyes and a scarlet slash of a mouth. It was nothing much out of the way for this kind of party, but she got immediate attention. Barbarossa stopped short in mid-bellow and then announced, "By God, as I live, the Contessa di Lampedusa." I turned away; things were getting odd again, I thought, and at the same time the barman murmured, "Signor," and pushed a fresh Bourbon towards me; which I felt ought not to be wasted at these prices.

Somebody said, "Cut it out, Heine you fool," and when I looked round again there was a powerfully built individual in a dinner-jacket leaning heavily on Barbarossa's shoulder, while two of the waiters were shepherding the lady away to a table. "Your bouncer?" I asked the nice barman, and he shrugged, and I nodded gravely and was just about to say that it was all done with impeccably good taste when I became aware of two more appearances further down the bar. This time the cameraman again and Angela Caterina, now very pretty and more or less fully dressed once more in a gay little off-the-shoulder number; and also apparently in a forgiving mood, for she smiled and waved at me. All things considered that was very reconciliatory of her, I thought, and the least I could do would be to go and express my appreciation. But although the removal of Red Beard and his playmates had left a certain amount of space and quiet there still seemed to be a fair number of bodies between us, and before I could start to plot a course through them my elegant young Italian friend came back.

He said, "Hi there again. I've located Piretti. Seems he's over on the Lido; got quite a party set up there. What d'you say? Care to come over and join us?"

I examined the proposition carefully from all its angles, and then asked, "Why not?"

SEVEN

"The name's Jo," he said, and he had a little boat in the public moorings at San Marco. It was a nice night for a short walk, and plenty of light and people about on the waterfront; but once out of the illusory atmosphere of Harry's Bar realism was starting to reassert itself. Knowing the capacity of these people for arranging events quickly this was probably going to be the most insane thing I had ever done. The only rational course now was to say, "Thanks a lot, Jo, but not tonight." But I couldn't do it. Without any evidence for the idea I was still convinced that Alberti must have a man tailing me somewhere, and I had taken an intense dislike to this over-confident smart boy; the whisky had left me sober enough now, but bloody-minded. I had to find out what was due to happen on Saturday, less than two days away, as this was Thursday night; and I wanted to look at his boat.

That much at least was easily settled when he led the

way out along the planking. It was certainly not the one which had tried to sink us. As he had said, it was a little boat; small but, like himself, expensive and rather flashy in mahogany and crome with car seats for four in the cockpit. He dropped in behind the wheel and stood there swaying lightly as it rolled, looking up at me. "On our way then?" he asked.

This was the last moment when I might have told him what he could do with himself, but the faint grin and unmistakable challenge were too much for me. I said again, "Why not? It's smarter than the ferry and cheaper than a taxi."

He turned over the motor and we idled out away from the lights. Then three more people emerged from the crowd, getting into another boat; two men and a girl, so it looked as if Angela Caterina and the cameraman might also be coming to join the party. They seemed to be having trouble getting started, but I lost them for a minute as a *motoscafi* packed with passengers swept by uncomfortably close to us, and when that had passed I thought I caught sight of the tall woman, the rather improbable contessa, waving for a taxi. It was difficult to be sure of anything in the flash and glitter of the reflections, rolling unpleasantly and slapping in the water, and I asked, "What are we waiting for? You'll get us run down. Surely they know where we're going, don't they?"

We started to move slightly faster, heading out into the open though still only just cruising, and apparently he had noticed the contessa too, for he said, "I've never seen that dame in Harry's before. Do you know her?"

Why not, I wondered. A little improvisation might not do any harm; it might even start to get him about half as worried as I was myself. "I know of her, if it's the same woman. Claudia Lampedusa; Rome, Paris and New York. I don't think you're big enough to play in her league, Jo."

We were keeping well down out of the ferry-boat lanes, edging towards the island of San Giorgio Maggiore, and he was looking back over his shoulder, trying to pick up the lights of the other boat. It was a lot of black, empty water; much more than it looked in daylight, I thought, while he muttered, "I've never heard of her. What d'you mean?"

"She and her old man have the sort of connections that I wouldn't like to get my own fingers caught in. If you're trying to get in on the Ca' Silvestro business they might just laugh at you and tell you to run home to bed, or they might get irritated and slap you."

He was getting uncertain. Perhaps not so much by the gorgeous contessa as because he was missing his friends, starting to suspect that I had come along with him far too easily and beginning to look for the catch. He said, "I can't make out whether you're very smart or a sucker. Or just pissed."

There was no harm in letting him think that as well. "Just pissed," I told him. "But I'm not worried. I'm the only one who doesn't have to be. And for God's sake if we're going to a party why don't we go? It'll be all over before we get there."

He looked back over his shoulder again; still apparently without any sign of the other boat, for he muttered, "The bastards have let me down."

"Of course they have," I agreed. "I'd say the contessa's got them." They were amateurs, I thought; I might just as well give them the sort of story-line that amateurs would expect to hear. "She never goes far without her strong-arm boys. Neither do I unless I've got cover somewhere."

"You?" He stared at me. "You're just a goddam artist."

"That; and other things. I've been other things for a long time. What d'you think I was called in for?" In fact I wished I knew myself, but I added, "Be a big boy now. You're working yourself into a corner, Jo."

He was quiet for a minute, lining the boat round on the neon lights of Maria Elizabetta as if half making up his mind about something; slightly confused, and I could well understand it. Then he suggested, "We could do a deal."

"We might. But I don't see what you've got to offer. You can't cut me in on the deal because you don't have the property yet. And you're never likely to get it with the Lampedusas in the market."

"That's what you think." It was unpleasantly confident again. "The old bitch Silvestro is holding out on us so far, but we shall get it by the week-end. If we don't there'll be one hell of a blow-up."

"The contessa will have it by then. And if there is a blow-up you'll blow with it, won't you?"

"Don't fool yourself." He grinned at me. "There are lots of people about who don't exactly love Mama Silvestro. Two or three groups who could carry the can; and the cops will be only too glad to fix something on any one of them. There could be nice business in that too."

"It's a good idea." In fact I thought it was so full of loopholes that it was terrifying. I looked at the lights of the Elizabetta. They were steadily coming closer, and so far as I could see there was still no sign of the other boat. I just had to keep him talking for another ten minutes or so, and went on, "I'll tell you this much. I'm not too happy about it myself. Even from their angle it's all highly illegal; so you can guess what they want me for."

He was a quick, clever boy; you only had to suggest something to him and he picked it up at once. "They want you to take it out of Venice?"

I nodded. "That's right. But they're being too cagey. They haven't even shown me the thing yet. And until I've seen it and I know exactly what the job involves

I'm sitting on the fence."

He fell into it like a kitten into a bowl of cream. "It's a roll; about seventy centimetres long by twenty thick. They have to get some of it softened first before. . ." He stopped suddenly, prickling with suspicion. "They must have told you that much."

"Of course they've told me," I said quickly. "I just like to be sure everybody's telling the same tale, that's all." There was barely more than two hundred yards to go now; I could see the landing-stages, people walking in the light on the front and sitting at café tables across the road, and I asked, "So who told you? Angela Caterina? And who's the boss; who do I have to do a deal with? Is that Angela Caterina too?"

"Angie? Jesus! We don't have a boss; except. . . You'll have to do a deal with all of us."

Very confused now, I thought. "That's going to be rather difficult," I pointed out mildly. "They don't seem to be coming. What's wrong with Angie, anyhow?"

"She's nuts." He was getting angry. "She's starting to be a nuisance. We're going to have to do something about Angie soon."

"Like you did something about Antonello?"

But that was a mistake. He started so violently that he jerked the wheel over. The boat lurched round wildly, and he whispered, "My God! What do you know about that? Listen, you. . ."

"You listen instead," I cut in. "And take it easy. I don't give a damn about Antonello. He's not my business, and so far I'm prepared to leave it that way. But I know enough to make life awkward for all of you if I have to. So now for God's sake stop fooling about and run this thing in. I'm getting thirsty again. Let's go and have a drink and start talking seriously."

There was not much more than another hundred yards to go now, and he was badly shaken. I was sweating myself; it was still a lot of water. He muttered, "You're a bastard; you can't be so smart as all that," and I said, "I haven't really started trying yet." But at that moment a headlight stabbed out from the darkness behind us.

Jo turned again, grinning suddenly, showing his teeth in the glare from the shore. He said, "You're not so smart." yelled back, "What kept you?" flung the boat into a tight, sickening curve and opened the throttle. The swing and the sudden lift half threw me out, realising that if I hit the water now it would be like hitting a stone wall, glimpsing the shore lights streaming past through a sheet of spray, and I hauled myself back by clinging to the dashboard grip and clawing at the seat. We seemed to be racing along parallel with the coast road, bouncing and plunging, but the lamps were swinging off again, and I pulled myself close enough to shout in his ear, "Slow it, you bloody idiot. You'll smash us both."

He laughed, showing off again, and I tried to reach past him to get at the ignition switches, but he jabbed viciously with his elbow, twisted the wheel one-handed into another heeling turn, and for the second time I barely saved myself. He yelled, "Keep still, or I'll have you out."

There was nothing else I could do at that speed while he had the wheel, and I braced myself back in the seat, watching him. The headlight behind us flicked off as suddenly as it had stabbed out, but you could see the other boat clearly now; and at the same time the lamps on the shore tailed away into darkness. We were racing south along the inside shore of the Lido, where there was a long stretch of deserted beach facing tidal sand-banks in the least-frequented part of the lagoon, and I began to see what he was planning and shouted at him, "You're a fool, you know. That's a police launch. They've been tailing me for days."

He laughed again. He asked, "Who're you trying to bluff? You're not so smart, brother. I'll tell you something now. You got the names mixed. I'm Piretti; *Jo* Piretti. Toni's driving the other boat; Toni Donato. I guess you're going to do some talking now." He reached forward deliberately and cut the motor, at the same time switching on our own headlamp, and we settled in the water, losing way quickly. Ahead of us there was a low, gravelly sand-bank, half wreathed in mist, and he said, "It's as good a place as any for a party.

The other boat was overtaking quickly as we slowed, and if I had ever had any vague hopes that it might really be a police launch they were disappointed, for I could see Angela Caterina leaning out, and she called, "Have you got him, Jo? Our engine wouldn't start." Jo waved back with one hand, standing now and reaching down to the wheel, concentrating on edging into the bank, but we were still moving fairly fast. He lurched as we struck the gravel, and at the same time I swung up from the seat and hit him hard at the back of his neck. I dislike violence; I even hoped briefly that I had not hit him too hard, but as he fell I shouldered him out of the boat and got myself behind the controls.

There, however, my hundred to one chance of luck gave out. I got the motor started, but at the best I had only a few seconds, and I could not find the reverse. I merely succeeded in driving the thing harder into the shingle, and by that time the others were on me. There was only one thing left to do; get on to the sand, fast. It was hard enough underfoot, though wet and slimy with seaweed, and there seemed to be no more than a few square yards of it, barely above water. They were out as soon as I was myself; little Angela with the mist swirling about her in the reflected light from the headlamp, fantastic with her pretty face and her impudent little party dress, the bearded cameraman, and the other one Jo had said was Toni Donato; light coloured slacks, a monogrammed shirt and a silk scarf. Another smart boy, and by the look of him he would probably be the worst, I decided; as I also realised that I had not hit Jo anything like hard enough, for he was already dragging himself out of the water too.

They stood watching me, apparently waiting for Donato to move. It seemed like half an hour. Then Angela whispered, "Beat the bastard up. I want to see it.

I was wrong, I thought sickly; Angela was the worst. Donato said, "Don't be impatient, sweetie; all in good time. You shall stamp on his face in a minute. Has he hurt you, darling?" he asked Jo. Jo was groping in the boat. He came up with a short bar of some sort, and Donato said, "No, dear, not that. We don't want any nasty people asking questions when they find him, do we?"

That seemed to startle Angela. She was obviously high on something, but she started, "No, Toni. You promised just to. . ."

"Be quiet, sweetie," he told her. "You're a big girl now." He spoke with a slight lisp, smiling at me pleasantly. "He must admit we did warn him."

My own voice surprised me. I expected it to be a hoarse croak, but it sounded perfectly normal. "That's right; you did warn me." I was listening. I thought I could hear another boat somewhere, and I had to keep them talking. "That's why I came to look for you tonight. I told Jo. I'm open for a deal."

"My dear, what sort of a deal?" he asked. "You're such a frightfully rude and inquisitive person; we simply don't want you about."

Angela started to say something, badly frightened now, but Jo came in with a rush, trying to get behind me, and I swung round to face him. He slipped in the slime underfoot and I hit him again as he stumbled, but the other two were on my back with Donato saying, "Hold him, George dear." One of them got his forearm round my throat, and then it was just murderous confusion. All I could do was to try to protect my face and head, and kick or hit out blindly when I got the chance. I could feel the blood thumping in my ears, fighting for breath and retching on the sour aftertaste of whisky; I heard Jo whispering obscenities, Donato laughing, and the other grunting with agony as somehow I got in one vicious blow. Angela screamed, "Stop it!" She seemed to be a long way off. But then, apparently quite close and distinctly I heard the sound of another boat; and a sharp, spitting crack.

Angela screamed again; one of them asked, "For God's sake, what's that?" and they broke away. I was left swaying slightly, dimly aware of them backing off and the sudden silence, breathing heavily and blinking incredulously at what appeared to be a final grotesque unreality. Black water rippling up over the sand and a wreath of mist, the two boats and now one more close in; the tall woman in the purple and gold caftan standing in it, picked up in the glare of Jo's headlight with a small glittering pistol in her hand. There were two men half visible behind the windshield, the normal taxi crew, but we were all staring at the woman, frozen. Angela whimpered softly; Donato started, "Who the hell. . ?" But she jerked the pistol at him. She said coldly, "Keep still, all of you. I want Hedley. The rest of you, the first one who moves. . ."

None of them tried to stop me. I walked away, gathering my wits. It was too improbable, I thought vaguely, getting comic again; and that frightened me almost more than the fight itself. She could not possibly hold them for more than another few seconds and it seemed a long way to Jo's boat, but I stopped there deliberately, took out the ignition key and tossed it into the water. One of them did move then for I heard his feet crunch on the gravel, and she snapped, "I said to keep still." She added to me, "Be quick," and I climbed into the other boat and pushed it off to drift across the few yards to the taxi. Donato started to splash down then but stopped at another jerk of the pistol, and I took out his key too, flung that away and fell into the taxi.

I was still half dazed, only just realising who the woman was. "Now let's go," she ordered crisply. Our motor started up, and I caught one last glimpse of the other boats and figures splashing out helplessly after them; then we were roaring back towards the lights. Our driver seemed to want to get out of the area as quickly as possible. He muttered, "*Mama mia, signora*, what is this?" and she asked, "What did it look like?" She said, "Don't you ever let me see you do anything so mad and reckless as that again, Paul Hedley. You had me very worried. And by the look of you what you need now is some very, *very* strong black coffee."

A quarter of an hour later and we were sitting in one of the big, popular café-bars on the Viale Elizabetta, where we were less likely to attract attention in the late-night crowd. Judith had wanted to come here so that she could find a ladies' room to let down her hair to its usual style and take off the make-up before going back to the Pensione Martinelli. One could hardly blame her; as she said, she might have found it embarrassing to have to explain who she was. She was wearing her spectacles again, and the exotic caftan was now simply a very attractive dress. The rest of the effect, she explained kindly, was merely a pair of high-heeled shoes. She was nicely pleased with herself—probably far too pleased, I thought, considering what we had left behind on that sand-bank—

and she chuckled happily. "I came in here to start with to do my hair up and put that face on. It was really quite something, wasn't it? One of the waiters nearly fell down when he saw me."

I said, "I'm not surprised."

"But of course I haven't ever told you that I used to be quite a star in amateur dramatics at high school. Though that was a long time ago."

"You've obviously had a life full of incident. And you haven't lost your touch. You were an instantaneous first-night success."

"The Contessa di Lampedusa," she murmured. "Isn't that nice? I wonder, is there such a person?"

"I've no idea. I doubt it. I'd say that exhibitionist idiot in Harry's was just trying to be funny." She tried the title over again, and I went on, "You might as well know your other name. You're Claudia."

"Am I?" She appeared to be delighted. "That's nice too. But why?"

I told her about the story I had put across to Jo Piretti in the boat. "It seemed to be a good idea to confuse him a bit," I finished. "He seems to be a gullible type; not nearly so smart as he likes to think he is. Piretti's nothing. It's the other one who's vicious; Toni Donato. He's the one who loosed off that little trick in the church this morning."

She stared at me. "How do you know that?"

"Bits and pieces I picked up. The two halves of his name. One from little Angela and the other from Piretti. Piretti gave quite a lot away." I told her about that too, and then said, "I'm sorry, Judith, but we've got to finish it. We can't risk any more. We've got to turn it over to Alberti."

She nodded unwillingly, watching the endless promenade outside on the avenue. "I suppose so. It seems a pity though; like giving in. And there's so much hangs on it. Your Isola San Giorgio friends to say the least. And Mrs Messina-Silvestro."

"I know well enough what hangs on it," I told her, perhaps rather more sharply than was really necessary. "A roll of Leonardo da Vinci cartoons or sketches. Let's say five million dollars or more. And I've a fair idea of what Mrs Messina-Silvestro is planning. She badly needs money for her restoration and repair work, but I doubt if anybody in Italy could offer anything like that for what the government might claim belongs to the state anyway. So they have to be smuggled out and sold either in Germany or America; after you, Kleber, d'Espinal and probably one or two more experts have established their provenance and guaranteed that they're authentic. But the whole thing is highly illegal, and you all know it. I'd say that under Italian law it's an active criminal offence. So if the police or any other authorities pick up so much as a hint of the discovery the deal has to be off even before it gets started. That's what hangs on it; and I see your point of view. But it's getting too dangerous."

She flushed brilliantly; and angrily. "If you must talk about this in public please talk quietly. The 'deal', as you call it, is nothing to do with me; and Hans Kleber and Sir Harcourt d'Espinal are simply working out of friendship for Mrs Silvestro. But none of us can see why an old lady should not be allowed to sell her own family property where and how she pleases. Can you? Could it be," she asked, "that you are just the slightest bit scared?"

One way and another it had been an irritating day, and I held on to my own temper with an effort. "You're dead right, I'm scared. I'm scared for you and Kleber. And I'm scared for myself and Mrs Silvestro. Listen, Judith, I wouldn't go so far as to say that these people are nuts, but they're certainly incalculable. They do things on the spur of the moment. The girl's bored and off balance. Donato's more than half psychotic. He's like a lot more people around these days; convinced that what he wants to happen has to be *made* to happen. And after tonight. . ."

"And might I ask who started tonight?" she enquired. "Who went to that bar and got slightly drunk? And *very* reckless." She stopped short suddenly; just in time. "I'm sorry, Paul. I shouldn't have said that. I'd hate us to quarrel. But will you tell me just one thing? Hans Kleber and I have both been wondering. Do you represent any other party?"

"You mean somebody else in the market? The answer is no. Quite definitely I do not. There's a friend of mine interested; my agent. But that's only because he's curious. He heard a whisper on the grapevine that something was going to turn up in Venice. He doesn't command that sort of money; and in any case Leonardo is right out of his field."

"Thank you," she said gravely. "You do understand, don't you? You've always seemed to know just a little too much."

"Only what you and other people have told me."

"Yes. You're clever, Paul. You add things up very quickly. I suppose it was my mentioning Queen Christina that put you on to it?"

"Queen Christina of Sweden and a balloon seller taken together would make almost anybody inquisitive, don't you think?" I asked. "Let's stick to the subject, Judith. I'm going to call Alberti; tonight. I'll tell him as little as possible, of course."

"I don't see how you can avoid telling him everything." She sighed faintly. "I suppose you wouldn't care to wait until you've had a chance to take a careful look at the other pictures in the Ca' Silvestro?"

"What have they got to do with it?" I asked.

"I'd just like you to take a look at them first." She got up suddenly. "Shall we go then?"

We walked up slowly to the end of the Elizabetta and stood watching the last ferry trailing its reflections across the black water. There were very few people aboard, none at all on the lower deck at the stern, and the association of ideas was inevitable. She shivered suddenly and said, "It's quite horrid, but is there any chance that those people will . . . drown out there?"

"Not the slightest. It might save everybody a lot of trouble if they did," I added callously. "They'll wade or swim after their boats and get them started without the keys. But they'll be wet and cold; and vicious. They won't be in the mood to be put off by a toy pistol again."

"Oh dear," she murmured, "you notice everything, don't you? I thought a woman like the character I had in mind just wouldn't go anywhere without a pistol in her handbag. And there's a store down the end of the Elizabetta called The Westerner Saloon. They sell everything from Stetsons to six-shooters." We turned off towards the Via Lepanto and the pensione, and she went on, "There were two calls for you after you left. Sir Harcourt d'Espinal first. I told him you had mentioned something about a near miss accident but you hadn't appeared to think it was anything serious. And then your friend in London. He asked me to tell you that he'd express mailed the research agency's report, and you should have it tomorrow."

We were at the pensione then, and I pushed open the glass doors for her. "You've had quite a busy evening, haven't you?" I asked. "And I haven't thanked you properly yet."

"You don't have to. It's been something quite unusual; I've really enjoyed it." She looked at me levelly. "It's a pity it has to end so disappointingly, isn't it? Good night, Paul."

The last word, I thought, as she took her key and disappeared up the stairs without looking back. The

Martinelli at the reception was sympathetic again as he gave me mine, and I said, "That's the way it goes. Will you give me an outside line?" I asked. "I want to make a call; from my room."

There was the slightest hint of reproach, a glance at the clock, and I nearly enough told him to leave it until tomorrow; one of those moments when you feel that everything may hang on a few words, but I turned away towards the stairs and then stopped again by the open archway to the lounge. The priest was sitting there reading, with the blue cat sprawled luxuriously asleep on his knees, and he looked up as I paused, smiling pleasantly and saying, "This beautiful little creature lords it over the entire establishment. One is unwilling to disturb him."

I said, "Yes . . ." wondering briefly whether he had actually been waiting up to see Judith come in. The fingers holding his book were very clean but slightly stained with something, and I had never seen him smoking. It was a sudden guess. I went on, "Dr Harford hasn't introduced us yet, Father; so I suppose I shouldn't ask. But I imagine that softening ancient canvases from a roll must be a very difficult operation. At nearly five hundred years old it could be almost impossible. How is it going?"

If he was surprised he showed no sign of it. He spoke in English, but with a trace of French accent. "It's certainly a very delicate task. It needs a great deal of patience. But it can be done." He got up, carefully removing the cat. "I'm Jérôme Bonnard, by the way. And I had no idea how late it is. Shall we let it go at that, Mr Hedley?"

Once up in my room of course I should have got straight on to the telephone. It was merely common sense. All I had to do was simply tell Alberti that the people he was looking for were Piretti, Toni Donato and a man they called George; and that something was due to happen on Saturday. But it was obvious that he already knew that; and equally obvious that just giving him three names would only be the beginning. Judith was quite right; I should have to tell him everything. I thought of the look in her eye when I met her in the morning; and I thought of Mrs Messina-Silvestro, Emilia Pentecost and d'Espinal. Hedley the heel, I thought, scared stiff of a crazy girl and a bunch of amateurs; and it was possible even that we had frightened them off tonight. In fact I knew with cold, chilling certainty that the absolute reverse was far more likely. Donato would be really dangerous now; and I had a suspicion that there might be other people, as yet unknown, behind him.

We could not risk it, I told myself. It looked as if they changed their plans as one or another of them had a fresh idea, and we had no means of knowing what they might try next. Yet on the other hand Judith's hints about the other pictures at the Ca' Silvestro, taken in conjunction with the costs of the restoration work there and Emilia Pentecost, could only mean one thing; and nobody would thank me for opening up that sort of scandal, least of all Emilia and Mrs Messina-Silvestro. It was a damnable decision to have to make, and I was still undecided when the telephone buzzed softly.

Young Martinelli murmured that he was waiting to lock up and put the lights out; did the signor still wish to make his outside call? I said, "I'm sorry to have kept you waiting, Stefano. Forget it. It's getting too late."

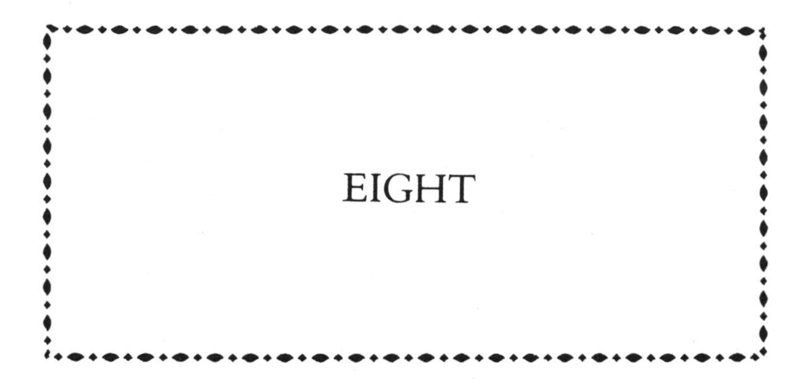

EIGHT

Still more than half convinced that we should have turned it over to the police I was down early next morning, but apparently Judith had been even earlier, for Graziella was already clearing away the inevitable orange juice glass and half-finished Melba toast. She said, "Oh yes, signor, some little time since. She took her breakfast with the Father, and then went out very quickly. She was displeased about something, polite as always, but plainly displeased." In one of her severe and academic moods, I thought, with Paul Hedley well out of favour; and it might create fresh complications if she had gone off to do something herself under the impression that I had talked to Alberti. After last night I wouldn't put anything past her.

There was a bulky envelope on my plate; so the Italian mail was also early, almost miraculous. Five or six photo-copied pages of close typescipt and a note from Manny Levin. "You might make more out of this than I can," he wrote, "but it looks as if we've got it wrong somewhere. All of the most important items are accounted for except the lost Cellini pieces, and it can't be either of those; the wrong people interested. All the same I ran into Gregor Kelnikoff in Bond Street yesterday — d'Espinal's Paris associate — and he was full of hints. I wouldn't have talked so much myself. The art discovery of the century he said, but it seems he's worried about another interest somewhere; somebody in Milan. Fishing to know if I'd heard anything about that on the vine. I told him I had not and not likely to, but the only man in Milan is Piretti and I know that old crook — who doesn't? — so I called him. Fresh surprise. His secretary said that *Signor Piretti nonno* is in Porec — which is just inside Yugoslavia — and not expected back until mid next week. So will you tell me what a man of Piretti's age does in a place like Porec? It s just I'm inquisitive. How's the portrait going?"

He had marked several paragraphs of the research agency report, but I left that to read later. It was then half-past eight, and there was a lot to do if I was to get back here in time to pick up the Ca' Silvestro boat just before eleven. First of all a note for Judith, and I said, "I have not spoken to A, and now agree with you it may be best to forget this; certainly for the present." I went on, "What about our lunch-date with Dr Kleber? Hope to be back here by ten-thirty. Otherwise at the Ca' Silvestro from eleven to twelve as usual; when I will try to get a look at the pictures there. And I'm sorry that last night finished so disappointingly too." At least conciliatory, I thought.

Next a quick look at the map in the reception and a short call to San Giorgio Piccolo. As Manny had said, Porec was only a little way over the Italian-Yugoslav frontier, and more importantly the nearest place to Venice; about sixty miles away, an easy run for any average motor-cruiser. It was all adding up fast now, I thought, while Martinelli dialled for me, and when Emilia Pentecost came on I said, "Sorry to be so sudden, Emilia, but I want to talk to you and d'Espinal. I'm coming out to you right away."

She was not noticeably enthusiastic. She asked, "Isn't it rather short notice? Harry has to go across to San Francesco." I had the impression that she felt she had given something away, for she stopped and then went on, "I mean we're always glad to see you, of course; but wouldn't this afternoon be more convenient?"

"I don't think so," I told her. "I'm trying to be helpful, Emilia. I'll be with you a bit after nine."

There was just time for Manny's research notes in the taxi, although I had to skip most of the life of Christina of Sweden, which took up several pages; 'A fascinating and brilliant woman,' they said. But I was looking for information about her pictures, in particular anything by Leonardo, or any possible connection however tenuous with the Ca' Silvestro; and towards the end one sentence fairly leapt out at me. 'In Rome she was closely associated with Cardinal Giancarlo de' Medici (1655) possibly one of his long succession of mistresses.' And Judith, I remembered, had said that Giancarlo was one of Mrs Messina-Silvestro's distant ancestors.

It was the same with the list of items in her art collections. Manny's agency had done its work well, and there was too much to study in detail, but again two paragraphs stood out. 'Leonardo da Vinci. *Leda and the Swan*, attributed to. This work is in the Spiridon Collection, Rome, and is still the subject of considerable controversy. Expert opinion is about evenly divided as to whether it is by Leonardo or not. The flesh tones and the sensuous handling of the figure, in particular the enigmatic smile—which resembles that of the *Mona Lisa*—are said to be entirely typical of this master, but the other details and background are unlike his normal technique. Leonardo himself wrote (the *Treatise on Painting*) "It came to pass that I executed a painting for a lover. He wished to see the features of his goddess mirrored so that he might kiss them without arousing suspicion Yet conscience vanquished his voluptuous sighs, for he constrained himself and put her out of the house."

'The lover in this case was Giuliano de Medici, and the *Leda* is a nude portrait of the mistress whom he abandoned on his marriage to Philisberta of Savoy (1515) as he also gave back the picture itself to Leonardo. A *Leda and the Swan* later passed into the possession of Queen Christina (there were several copies made in the intervening hundred years or so) and she claimed to have indisputable proof that this was the authentic work by Leonardo da Vinci. The exact nature of this proof however has never been known.

"Until now?" I asked myself as the boat swept round to the San Giorgio landing-steps. "Is that what they've got; the original cartoons and trial sketches?" It was not surprising that everybody was so cagey, I thought; and five million dollars was a very modest estimate.

Emilia and d'Espinal were waiting for me; a Roman emperor contemplating something distinctly unpleasant again. He said, "One would not wish to be discourteous, my dear fellow. But I hope this is important. I understood that your manner was somewhat peremptory."

"It wasn't meant that way." And best to let him have it straight and hard. "Unless you want a lot of trouble over the Leda cartoons it's extremely important."

It was startling how wolfish d'Espinal could appear suddenly. "God's faith, Hedley," he breathed, "what do you know about the cartoons? And what the devil are you up to?"

"Harry!" Emilia cut in warningly. There were garden seats by the balustrade, placed to command a view of the lagoon and the distant shimmer of Murano and Venice, a few red-sailed fishing-boats drifting idly across the blue silk. "Let's sit down and talk this out calmly," she suggested. "You'd better start by telling us why you are so interested, Paul."

"I certainly will," I promised. "And then I'd like to know what you're setting me up for. But we'll take the cartoons or whatever they are first. A roll about seventy centimetres long by twenty in diameter; discovered in the Ca' Silvestro in the course of the restoration work there; at least one canvas which has to be softened before it can be opened out, and other items. Is that correct?"

D'Espinal muttered something under his breath. As far as possible with his chin sunk on his chest he nodded. "They were found in a cupboard which had been panelled over; probably in the early eighteenth century. Two trials, lightly painted on canvas; four cartoons in red chalk on paper. Preliminary essays to show the client." He grinned at me rather mirthlessly. "Much as you prepared several sketches for Mrs Messina-Silvestro."

"And she'd have been far from pleased if they had been anything like these," Emilia murmured drily.

D'Espinal nodded again. "To say the least they're surprising. Especially for Leonardo. You can appreciate that the story of Leda and the Swan lends itself to some astonishing visual interpretations. That is probably why they were put away in a cupboard and forgotten."

"But I imagine that will considerably increase their value?"

"Very considerably," He pouted distastefully, almost prudishly. "It will also cause a great deal of controversy."

"So that's why you or Mrs Messina-Silvestro called Dr Hans Kleber in? To authenticate your own findings. And he asked for Dr Judith Harford of Boston for a further opinion?" Emilia laughed softly. I fancy that she got a certain amount of affectionate amusement out of d'Espinal, although he looked at me wickedly. I went on, "I suppose the provenance is through Cardinal Giancarlo de Medici? He acquired the cartoons from Christina of Sweden, and they passed from him to the Silvestro family?"

D'Espinal exploded. "I don't know what you're driving at. It may be a merely vulgar display of knowledge. I hope it is. But I must advise you, my dear fellow, that you're overstepping the bounds of courtesy."

"I hope not. I just want to get it all quite clear. It's time somebody did. And I've told you, I want to know what you've set me up for. We'll come to that in a minute. There are one or two other points first; including a Father Jérôme Bonnard at the Pensione Martinelli. I'm guessing that he's a Jesuit; some of the fathers of the Society are experts in quite a lot of fields. I take it that he's working on the canvases for you?"

D'Espinal appeared to be speechless, but Emilia nodded calmly. "He is. Don't look so thunderous, Harry. Either we have to trust Paul or come to terms with him. And what next?" she asked me.

This really could cause an explosion. But there was no point in being evasive about it. I went on deliberately. "The pictures in the Ca' Silvestro. I haven't had a chance for more than a glance at them in passing, but I know a Verdizzotti of the School of Titian when I see it. There's a Manetti, and a Padovanino; and at least one of the School of Siena." I paused. "I suggest they're forgeries."

I did not look at d'Espinal, but Emilia turned pale,

staring at me, and then snapping, "*Copies!* Damn you, you are getting a nuisance now."

D'Espinal got up, massively polite. "I regret, Hedley, that in one more moment I shall toss you into the lagoon."

"And where will that get us?" I asked. "I'm simply suggesting that Mrs Messina-Silvestro has been selling off her private collection to pay for the reconstruction work, and you've been helping her."

Suddenly, surprisingly, Emilia laughed. "Harry, for Heaven's sake do stop being melodramatic. He knows so much we might as well tell him all of it."

There was a long, glowering pause before he grunted, "Very well. If you must know, fourteen pictures over the last three years or so. Just over a million pounds."

"Fourteen?" I repeated. "A million? You and Dr Kleber sold them?"

"Kleber is a very old friend of the family. Between us we placed them in Germany, America and France. Even one in Saudi Arabia." A slight touch of complacency there.

I looked across at the lovely old Italianate villa and the carefully tended garden, thinking of the whole peaceful little island. "You really are in a mess, aren't you?" I asked.

"If it comes out we're ruined," Emilia said flatly. "And so is all of this. Even if we don't face criminal charges."

"And all for the sake of helping an obstinate old woman," d'Espinal exploded again. "Very well, Hedley. What are your terms?"

"If you talk like that you won't be able to meet them," I told him. "I happen to like Mrs Messina-Silvestro. I've a weakness for autocratic old dragons, and so far as I'm concerned she's entitled to do what she likes with her own property. So now suppose you tell me what's due to happen on Saturday?"

"It may be a hoax," d'Espinal muttered. "We can only hope it is. Some person or persons unknown have threatened to destroy the Ca' Silvestro. To blow the place up."

"They've threatened to do what?" I enquired, although in fact I was not surprised. Piretti had told me plainly enough in the boat last night. 'Lots of people about who don't exactly love Mama Silvestro,' he had said. 'Two or three groups who could carry the can.' It was perfectly typical of the whole style of planning; and all the more dangerous for that reason.

"She received a letter last week, posted in Rome." Emilia explained. "It was really quite clever in its way. It gave her until this Saturday. She was to place an advertisement in the Venice newspaper, *La Gazzettina*, saying that she was prepared to relinquish Cardinal Giancarlo's bequest. She would then receive further instructions. If she refused to do that she was advised to remove herself and her household from the Ca' Silvestro to avoid unnecessary loss of life. The inference is quite obvious."

There was something which did not make sense, I thought. "And Mrs Messina-Silvestro called in the police? So she must have told them about the cartoons. Which is the last thing either you or these other people want."

"Paul, my dear," Emilia murmured, "surely you must know a little about Amelita Messina-Silvestro by now. Celia van Druyten called in the police. Amelita was furious. She told them she hadn't the slightest idea of what Cardinal Giancarlo's bequest is."

D'Espinal stirred uneasily. "It's the very devil of a dilemma. Neither have the police the slightest idea of anything. They never have. They say it's not characteristic of any of the well-known groups, but they're not sure. The Silvestros are supposed to have been supporters of Mussolini."

"That's a long time ago. Were they?"

He shrugged. "I doubt it. They're more likely to have despised him. But just the rumour is more than enough for some of the lunatics we have about today. Especially if they wish to find an excuse."

I said, "That's what they're doing. I can give you two names. There might be others behind them, but do these mean anything to you to start with? Jo Piretti and Toni Donato?"

D'Espinal stared at me, blinking like an owl in sunlight. "We know of them of course. But if you were to suggest that they're responsible nobody would believe you. One might not call them respectable. . ." He sneered visibly, obviously with his own ideas of what constitutes respectability. "But they're certainly well known. I doubt if either of them could even tell you what a Leonardo cartoon is. The Pirettis are millionaires. Milan and Turin I believe. The Donato family are property developers. Mestre and Porto Marghera."

Something which had been said at Mrs Messina-Silvestro's cocktail party rang a bell with me then; some extremely unpleasant remarks about property developers. But I let that go for the moment, and went on, "There's one of the Pirettis at least who must know what Leonardo cartoons are. An art dealer of some sort in Milan. He's referred to as the *Signor Piretti nonno*; the Piretti grandfather."

"Good God!" D'Espinal smacked his forehead with his open palm. "I imagined that old rascal was either retired or dead. Emilia, my dear, I've been grievously at fault. I never so much as thought about Luigi Piretti."

"You'd better think about him now," I suggested. "Because he's waiting at Porec in Yugoslavia. They're obviously going to run the cartoons across to him there. And he's expected back in Milan by the middle of next week. So that means they expect to have them in the next few days."

"You know young Piretti is a friend of Angela's?" Emilia asked quietly.

"Yes. I'm sorry."

She laughed shortly; rather jarringly. "You've no need to be. You can't tell us anything about Angela Caterina that we don't already know ourselves. I've been saying for years that eventually somebody will either have to strangle that girl or drown her."

"My dear," d'Espinal started to protest, but I asked, "Where are the cartoons now? San Francesco del Deserto?"

"How the devil do you know that?" he growled.

"It keeps cropping up. Kleber mentioned it yesterday for no apparent reason. It struck me that he wanted to see whether I reacted."

"It's a Franciscan monastery; the whole island," Emilia said. "It's very peaceful. Aunt Teestock and Mrs Messina-Silvestro are both friends of the Father Guardian. There couldn't be a safer place."

"And Kleber, Judith Harford and Father Bonnard are all there now, working on them?" D'Espinal grunted, and I enquired flatly, "Do we get together on this or not? If so I've got several suggestions to make. But we have to talk about them; and I must get back to the Lido to meet the Ca' Silvestro boat."

There was a lot to cover in all the events of the last few days, including Judith's charade last night and how it had ended. That seemed to amuse Emilia at least, especially the thought of Angela Caterina marooned on a sand-bank. She watched me rather quizzically, although d'Espinal grunted that it was a damned silly trick. "It worked," I pointed out. "And it gives us the background to what I'm about to suggest now."

I talked on for several minutes more. It was something I had thought of as I was getting up that morning, and this time when I finished he was distinctly more friendly. "It's ingenious," he admitted, "and it might be possible. Indeed it must be made possible. It will be damnably dangerous, but . . . My dear fellow, I cannot say how grateful. . ." He looked at Emilia. "Can you manage it, my dear?"

She nodded. "I think so. It gives me about twelve hours."

"Very well then." Imperial Caesar ordering the Praetorian Guard, I thought. "We can easily get half a dozen men from Torcello and Burano; more if necessary. Pietro has an army of brothers, cousins and nephews, and they are all exceedingly tough." The wolfish look appeared momentarily. "I can assure you that by midday nobody will land here or leave without permission. You do not anticipate any difficulty with Miss Harford?"

"She might have her own ideas; but I'm having lunch with her and Dr Kleber, and I think we can persuade her between us. That only leaves Angela Caterina. I suppose she got back here all right?"

Emilia shrugged. "Why shouldn't she? An hour or so in the lagoon wouldn't do that little bitch any harm; she can swim like a fish. In fact I heard a boat come in about one o'clock. She's probably still in bed."

"You'll keep her out of your studio?" I asked. "And you'll see that she doesn't slip across to Venice somehow?"

"Really, Paul," Emilia murmured, and d'Espinal announced, "My dear fellow, we know what we have to do. She will not even know that Emilia is in the studio; I shall contrive it that she hears me discussing your suggestion with Mrs Teestock, and she will be allowed to get at the telephone. For the rest, I've already told you that nobody will be allowed to land here or leave.

It's an excellent plan. I couldn't have conceived a better myself."

"We can only hope it works. So I'll get back now. You can tell me what you originally intended to set me up for when we have more time."

"Paul, my dear. . ." Emilia started, but then stopped short, looking back towards the house.

Angela Caterina must have been watching us, for she appeared suddenly in the windows on to the patio, coming across the grass. She looked extraordinarily beautiful, completely self-assured and smiling pleasantly; wearing coffee-coloured slacks and a cream shirt, tying a brilliant head scarf over her hair. She smiled at d'Espinal, but did not look at Emilia. They both stood quite still, watching her, and she said, "Hallo, you swine. I've got some nice messages for you and that contessa of yours. Are you going across? I'll come too, and tell you them on the way."

I had not so far realised that d'Espinal could be so menacing. He said, "No." Quite softly, but if I had been Angela Caterina I would have backed away from him.

"Why not, Harry dearest?" she asked; and then Emilia hit her. An open-handed slap to the face which went off like a pistol-shot in the quietness.

For a second or two the three of them remained frozen, as startled as I was myself. Then Emilia turned and walked away; Angela Caterina put her fingers up to her cheek like a shocked, aggrieved child, and d'Espinal asked coldly, "What did you expect?" I went down the steps to the boat without looking back and said to my driver, "Let's go, quickly."

It was an ugly little incident, and the impression it made, wondering what Angela Caterina might do now, whether we could even have another murder on our hands before long, hung over me all the way back to the Lido. Then at the pensione the note I had left for Judith was still in her keyhole in the reception. That was reasonable enough, I told myself; Judith was still out at San Francesco. But it left me with a vague premonition that things were going wrong for us, and half on an impulse I got young Martinelli to call the monastery for me. By this time the Ca' Silvestro driver was waiting for me, there was a long delay getting through, and then the boy finally murmured, "I'm sorry, Signor Hedley; they do not answer."

I had to go. It was impossible to put off the sitting at such short notice, and anyhow I wanted to talk to Mrs Messina-Silvestro. I said, "Try again, Benno. It's very urgent. I want a message to Signorina Harford. Tell her that I did not, repeat *did not* make a telephone call last night, and that it is most important we meet for lunch." He nodded brightly, probably imagining further steps in the romance, and I said, "I should be back here by twelve-thirty."

Inevitably I was late, and when we reached the Ca Silvestro at last there was a curious atmosphere there too. There were still two carabinieri outside, but the workmen seemed to have been withdrawn, and it was oddly silent. Carson admitted me, with a reproving look in his eye. He muttered, "It get on your nerves, this lot. An' I thought you was going to have a drink with me one of the nights?"

"Tonight," I promised quietly. "But I shall have to get away by ten o'clock."

Then as he marched ahead of me up the stairs his whisper floated back, "She ain't in the best of tempers this morning. Bit of a turn-up with *Miss* Celia van Druyten."

It was going to be a bad day; and although I had not noticed it until now it was getting stiflingly hot. The old building itself seemed tp pick up the heat, and for the first time I felt dissatisfied with the light on my canvas; it looked harsh and brassy. When Mrs Messina-Silvestro came in she was pale and tight lipped, more hawk-like than ever; you could feel the tension in her as she took up her pose while I prepared my palette. She said very little. I said almost nothing as I worked, or tried to work, and the house was uncannily quiet; the only sound was a telephone-bell ringing somewhere. It must have been nearly half an hour before the old lady broke the silence herself. "You are not in the mood for ugly old women today, Mr Hedley."

"I'm not in the mood for painting," I admitted. "It's not going well. That happens sometimes."

"Very well then, give it up." It was practically an order. "Let us talk instead. Sir Harcourt d'Espinal was speaking to me on the telephone earlier this morning. He informs me that you appear to know as much about our problems . . . our difficulties . . . as we do ourselves." Rather more in fact, I thought, but I did not say anything, and she went on, "He also tells me that you are prepared to go out of your way to help us; possibly at some risk to yourself. I wonder why? You do not strike me as being a particularly quixotic person."

"I hope not." It was difficult to tell her that it was because I had taken a liking to herself and Hans Kleber, rather more than a simple liking to Judith for however long that might last. "Probably personal motives. I've had trouble myself with some of the people concerned on the other side. They're reckless and vicious. And Miss Harford and your friend Dr Kleber are in considerable danger." I told her about the attempt to snatch Judith the other night. "There's no doubt that they intended to put up some other woman to impersonate her. It was a clever amateur's idea and they've almost certainly abandoned it by now. They seem to make plans and change them very quickly. That's what makes it so difficult. You can't tell what they might do next. But I think they'll try to kidnap and hold both Dr Kleber and Miss Harford."

"For what reason? As hostages?" She considered that for a minute. "In that case I should have to give in to them. For myself and my own property I would see them damned first. But for a fine man like Hans Kleber and this young American woman, both of whom are concerned only to do me a kindness . . . I should have no choice."

Even if she delivered the cartoons to them they would still plan to kidnap Kleber and Judith, I thought; they had to. But at this stage there was no point in worrying her as much as I was worried myself, and I asked, "Did Sir Harcourt mention any names to you?"

"He did. And he found it difficult to believe them. So do I. I know Antonio Piretti, for instance, and I dislike him intensely. I am no Socialist, thank God, yet even I can understand Socialism when I think of the way that man makes his money. But I'm certain he would not touch a thing like this. For one thing, he is too careful."

"His son might not be; working with the grandfather, Luigi Piretti. And the Donatos?"

"The Donato brothers are prominent in the faction which wants to rebuild Venice as a modern city; at an enormous profit. They propose very generously to preserve some of the special buildings as tourist attractions, but in the main they are planning a commercial terminal at the end of an autostrada from Milan. They say the place is doomed otherwise; merely a heap of flooded ruins sinking into the lagoon in less than twenty-five years." With an obvious effort she added, "They may be right. I merely refuse to see it that way. But I suppose they are honest people within their own lights; and, again, they would not touch this."

"And again the son might. I think I can even see why. May I put one very personal question. If the Ca' Silvestro were destroyed could you or would you rebuild?"

"Of course not," she said irritably. "First because I could not afford to. Second because it would be impossible. This house has been standing here for five hundred years, Mr Hedley. You cannot rebuild history."

And it would kill her, I thought. "And the site?" I asked.

"Would be comparatively worthless. Certainly of no interest to me. My executors would sell it for what it would fetch."

She sat staring out of the window for a minute; and then asked, "Can we stop them?"

"We can try. I still think the simplest method is to go straight to the police."

"And as soon as you mentioned those two names they would laugh at you more or less politely and show you the door." She smiled at me bleakly; obviously thinking that I was rather naïve.

"So we must do it our own way. Did d'Espinal tell you what I suggest?"

"He was very guarded. Naturally."

I could have wished that he hadn't been. It was coming up to twelve o'clock, and I wanted to get away, still with the worry at the back of my mind that things were going wrong. It took longer than I liked to explain again, but the old lady picked up the idea quickly enough, and when I finished she said simply, "It's ingenious. What do you want me to do?"

"Two telephone calls, both made so that they can be overheard here. One to d'Espinal, as soon as I leave, telling him that you have agreed to sell to the Contessa di Lampedusa. He's expecting that, and he'll understand it. The other to me at the Pensione Martinelli, about three o'clock this afternoon. It doesn't matter if I'm not there. In that case simply leave a message saying that you have arranged for the cartoons to be handed to me for delivery to the contessa tonight."

"Both so that they can be overheard?" she repeated. "Do you mean that someone actually in this house might be involved?"

She was visibly outraged, and I said quickly, "I mean it's a possibility. No more than that, but we must consider it. And I must go now. I must meet Dr Kleber and Miss Harford to tell them what we're doing. I want to get them safely out to San Giorgio this afternoon."

It was an awkward moment. I did not want any more explanations and did not have time for them. But fortunately then Carson arrived for the daily ritual of seeing me off the premises. The perfect butler once more; he announced, "There was a telephone, Mr Hedley; about half an hour ago. A Miss Harford. She wished not to disturb you, but requested me to say that she is unavoidably delayed, and cannot meet you for lunch."

There was no doubt about it now. Things were going very badly wrong.

NINE

I had more time than I wanted now, and water-taxis were starting to come expensive; and I wanted a drink. I went back to the Elizabetta on the ferry, trying to persuade myself that everything was perfectly normal; that young Benno Martinelli had put my message across to San Francesco and Judith had answered it simply by calling the Ca' Silvestro. She was having a peaceful day in a cool, quiet monastery; you could almost hear the chapel bell and the birds singing in the garden. It was a romantic thought, but totally unconvincing; and the heat was getting intolerable; a sky like brass and the lagoon a sheet of rolling lead. In the bar even the Venetian business men going across for lunch were down to their singlets, fanning themselves with their newspapers; and there was no ice. "Ice, signor?" the barman asked plaintively. "The machine itself is boiling."

At the Martinelli my note for Judith was still in the

reception; as it had to be of course, but I found myself wondering whether it had not been written about eight hours too late. Signora Martinelli was taking her turn behind the desk, and she murmured, "Is *caldo*, yes? *Mama mia*, we shall have a fearful storm; the only matter is when it will come." Benno was laying the tables languidly, but as soon as he saw me he broke into apologies. He seemed to feel that he personally was responsible for shattering the romance. He had tried, he protested. He had tried again, and again no answer. Then once more after that and at last he had got through, but this time the line had been so bad that one could scarcely hear a word. "You understand they are the religious, signor," he explained. "One cannot shout at them as one would others. I made my best to get the brother to understand. But. . ." He shook his head. "He was not very intelligent, and I doubt it."

"Don't get worried, Benno," I told him. "When was this?"

"It would be by then a little before twelve o'clock," he said.

About half an hour after Judith herself had called the Ca' Silvestro. And then even if she had got my message she would not have bothered to call again. It made sense, I thought.

But by half-past two, lying on my bed and sweating, I was convinced that it did not. We were up against the unpredictable again, and I knew now that I could not afford to wait any longer; I ought not to have waited this long. Five minutes later I was on the telephone to the Ca' Silvestro arguing with a sleepy and bad-tempered Carson. "I don't give a damn whether you like calls in the afternoon or not, I want Mrs Messina-Silvestro. Get her."

"Who the 'ell d'you think you are, cock?" he demanded, but I heard him speaking to Celia van

Druyten, and a second later she came on too, stating that Mrs Messina was resting, but I said, "She was going to call me herself at three o'clock. I'm just putting it forward by a few minutes. Now get her, please. It's about the Leonardo cartoons." And that, I thought, was guaranteed to keep both her and Carson listening.

More whispering in the background, and then the old lady asked, "Yes, Mr Hedley; what is it?" I said, "I'm afraid something might have happened. I want you to call the monastery at San Francesco. I understand the Father Guardian is a friend of yours. We have to know whether Dr Kleber, Miss Harford and Father Bonnard are still there. If not, what time did they leave and where did they go?"

"You think that might be serious?" she asked. "Very well; I'll call Father Andreas and come back to you."

Two forty-five then, and the temperature still climbing; so far as one could see from the window everything in sight seemed to be asleep in the brassy yellow glare. Ten to fifteen more minutes to wait before I could hope for an answer; just time to get a quick shower to cool off, clear my head and decide how to play it from here.

The telephone buzzed just as I was dressing again, and the old lady said crisply, "Father Bonnard is still there. But Hans Kleber and Miss Harford left just after twelve. Unfortunately it is not clear how they went; whether by the public *motoscafi* or taxi. Apparently there was some sort of message for Miss Harford. But the brother secretary who received it in the Father Guardian's office says the line was so bad that he could not make sense of it; except that someone had not done something last night. They told Father Bonnard they were meeting you for lunch." She paused, waiting for me while I thought that out, and then asked, "What do you propose to do?"

I said vaguely, "I'm not sure yet. We can only hope that somebody might try to contact me soon. Did you speak to Sir Harcourt d'Espinal this morning? About our arrangements tonight?"

"Yes, of course. I requested him to hand the cartoons to you, and told him you would deliver them personally to the Contessa di Lampedusa. Do you mean to keep to that in the light of this fresh development?"

"It seems to be the only thing we can do. I shall come over on the last ferry from this side. It leaves at eleven-thirty. And there's one other thing." I hesitated over this. If she lived up to her well-known reputation for obstinacy there was going to be an argument. "I think you and everybody else should evacuate the Ca' Silvestro; as soon as possible." There was a sudden, hard silence, and I went on, "Surely you must have considered leaving?"

She was starting to get irritated. "Tomorrow, perhaps. But only if it should seem absolutely necessary. Miss van Druyten and I are to go to Becky Kodaly. Carson has found accommodation for himself and the rest of our staff."

"It's absolutely necessary now," I told her. "These people are hurrying things up, and they're reckless. I know what at least one of them is planning to do, and what he hopes to get out of it." It was surprising she did not see it herself, I thought; she had as good as told me what it was in so many words this morning. I said, "Believe me, signora, I know how you feel. But. . ."

"I wonder if you do?" she interrupted. "But I am a self-willed old woman. Is that what you mean? Very well, Mr Hedley. We'll leave here as soon as possible."

And thank God for that at least, I breathed as I hung up.

I lay down on the bed, already starting to sweat again. Sooner or later somebody would get in touch with me; in the meantime there was nothing one could do but wait, and nothing to be gained by chasing blindly all over Venice and the lagoon looking for Judith and Hans Kleber. Short of some kind of lead that would be an impossible effort, and I had complete faith in Miss Harford's ability to look after herself and Kleber if she had to; especially if she were as angry as she ought to be by now. At this point my first essential was to rethink our own plans in the light of what Mrs Messina-Silvestro had told me today. We had not taken the instincts of a property developer sufficiently into account. There was a character named Crassus in ancient Rome who had amassed a huge fortune by waiting for building blocks to burn down and then moving in to buy the sites. He had never been known to set fire to any himself; but there is always room for improvements in technique.

It had been a bad morning, and it was a worse afternoon. Nothing at all happened. It always takes more nerve to wait than it does to rush about doing things, however illusory, and the telephone remained obstinately silent. By four-thirty my patience was starting to break, and I went down and round to Marco's for a cup of tea. People were just beginning to move again now although the heat seemed to be getting worse; there was just a chance that somebody might try to contact me at the bar. But by five o'clock there was still no sign of any approach, and then I rang the *Questura*. That was illusory too, for I did not think that Alberti would or even could do much in the few hours left to us, and he sounded considerably less than half interested. "Don't leave it too late," he told me. "I'm hoping to leave this damned place by six o'clock."

I was there by half-past five, and he was already preparing to go. "My God, this is wicked, isn't it?" he asked. "We're going to have one hell of a storm before long. I hope this is important. Or rather I hope it isn't."

"It depends on what you call important. I think it is. Dr Harford and Dr Hans Kleber have disappeared. They've been snatched."

"Really?" He had one eye on the clock. "When and from where?" I told him, very shortly, and he said, "Oh come now. Twelve o'clock and it's not yet six? They've gone for a trip somewhere. People just don't get snatched from San Francesco. It's not that sort of place."

"I'm suggesting that there was a taxi waiting for them. Or a boat which looked like a taxi. Try working this one out. I had a lunch-date with Miss Harford and Kleber, and when they left San Francesco at twelve o'clock they said they were meeting me. But half an hour before that there was a message received at the Ca' Silvestro to say that they could not make it."

He thought about that for a minute, but then murmured, "Yes; irritating for you. It doesn't amout to much though, does it? It might mean more if they haven't turned up by tomorrow."

"I'm suggesting that the people behind this are the people behind the Antonello murder."

"That wasn't a murder, you know. We're satisfied now that it was an accident. The man was as tight as a goldfish."

"It must have been an enchanting sight. And the little effort in the church the other day?"

"I'm afraid that was an accident too. We had the place examined, and the scaffolding there was damned dangerous. If it's any satisfaction to you the building foreman got the hell of a tear-off."

"I couldn't be more satisfied. So I'll make another suggestion. The same people are behind the bomb threat at the Ca' Silvestro."

"You've heard about that?" He shook his head. "We

know who's behind it. We know of two or three groups. Mrs Messina-Silvestro isn't at all popular, you know. This high-nosed aristocratic stuff doesn't go down well these days."

"And you want to fasten it on to one of those groups if you can? Politically useful? But you'll never make it stick; and I can give you two far better names. I'm taking a risk for several of my friends, telling you this, but things are getting out of hand. The boys you want are Toni Donato and Jo Piretti." For the first time I got a visible reaction out of him. He jerked upright on his chair, staring at me, and I went on, "Try picking one or both of them up and start asking questions. You might get some surprising answers."

"I should get something fall on my fingers so damned hot that I wouldn't be able to lick it off fast enough," he exploded. "god's sake, do you know who they are? Do you think I want to spend the rest of my life sweating it out in some dusty little hole in Calabria?" He glanced at the clock again pointedly. "See now, I don't want to hurry you, but I really think you ought to go back to the Lido and take it easy. I think this heat's starting to worry you a bit."

"It's not the only thing." We were getting round to my real reason for coming to see him. A calculated risk, but the way things were shaping now it had to be taken. I asked, "Do you still have a man tailing me?"

He laughed pleasantly. "Good Lord, no. Not for several days. As soon as we decided the Antonello affair was an accident I called them off. Orders from the Top Brass."

"Yes," I said. "The point is I rather feel I'm being made use of. Did you know that the workmen discovered something in the Ca' Silvestro? This lot called it 'Cardinal Giancarlo's bequest' in the letter they sent to the old lady. Do you know what it is?"

He had been tidying his papers away, and he

stopped suddenly, watching me. "No; I don't. But I've heard rumours, and I've been wondering. Mrs Messina say that bequest business is nonsense."

"Like hell it is. It's an art treasure of some sort, and God only knows how much it's worth. They've been keeping it out of the way somewhere, but they want me to bring it across from the Lido on the last ferry tonight. I gather that somebody else is going to take it out to Porec."

"Porec? In Yugoslavia?"

'That's right. I don't much like the idea; there's obviously a strong smell of fish about it. But I don't want to offend the old lady. She paying a lot for this portrait, and I've taken rather a liking to her."

He was still watching me, but he said, "Of course you don't want to offend her. So just carry on, and then tell me all about it tomorrow. Take my word for it, if this storm breaks nobody will be crossing to Yugoslavia while it lasts."

Don't overdo the simplicity, I thought. I went on, "I hope not. Because if they do Judith Harford and Kleber will go with them. And then somebody they've left behind will blow the Ca' Silvestro."

"My dear chap. . ." He sighed. "The Ca' Silvestro's been searched from top to bottom. It's a damned great warren of a place, but we're satisfied there's nothing there. That's a pity in a way. There are several ugly types we'd like to pull in for this."

"And you'd pull in the wrong people. Pick up Toni Donato and you'll settle the whole thing." I was starting to get angry, and I had to check myself. "Nobody's seen what's behind all this yet. I only realised it myself a few hours ago. We've all been thinking that the bomb threat was merely to induce Mrs Messina-Silvestro to hand over the Leonardo cartoons."

"So it's Leonardo cartoons is it?" He was very

interested this time. "That's big money in anybody's language. I wonder why nobody told us. And where are they now?"

"I don't know. I'm just picking them up and bringing them over at eleven-thirty. Let's stick to Toni Donato. The Donato family are property developers, and as property developers go they might even be quite respectable. But Toni is a bright young man. So far as he's concerned the Ca' Silvestro and the old lady are just a pair of ancient relics. So the Ca' Silvestro is destroyed, which is blamed neatly on the anarchists, he buys the site for peanuts out of his cut from selling the cartoons to Piretti's grandfather, and then sells it back to his family; who are looking for sites in Venice. It's a brilliant idea in its way."

"Brilliant," Alberti agreed. "And if it comes to ideas you're no slouch yourself. But I'd still like to know why nobody told us it's Leonardo cartoons."

"That's obvious, don't you think? You must know Italian law better than I do. Anyhow, they haven't been authenticated yet. But now somebody has told you, what are you going to do about it?"

"Tomorrow." He led me gently to the door. "Believe me, nothing is going to get very far tonight. I promise you that if Miss Harford and Dr Kleber haven't turned up by tomorrow we'll take the place apart for them. Though I'm quite sure you'll find she's waiting for you to buy her a nice cool drink when you get back to the Martinelli."

I thought it was more than doubtful. But at least I had used up another half an hour and got something out of it. It was fairly certain that he would have one man or more abroad that last ferry.

Half an hour used, but five and a half more yet to go and the problem of what to do with them. I got the long, cool drink first, trying to work out something useful, and then called the Martinelli. There was nothing there except that Sir Harcourt d'Espinal had called and wished me most urgently to get in touch with him; no other messages of any sort; Miss Harford had not returned and they had had word from Father Bonnard that he would not be in for dinner; and were they to expect me? Domestic life has to go on, I thought. I said, "I'm afraid not. But listen; this is important. If anybody wants to know where they can find me I shall be at Florian's from seven-thirty to eight-thirty. It doesn't matter who it is. Just tell them that, and see they get it clear."

D'Espinal next, and even on a bad line you could hear the alarm in his voice. Mrs. Messina-Silvestro had been on to him, and he asked, "For Heaven's sake, what is happening?"

I said, "I wish I knew."

I told him what I had done, and he whispered, "You've what? The police? Damn it, you had no authority for that. Do you realise what it may mean for all of us? And I understand you advised Mrs Messina to evacuate the Ca' Silvestro. Was that necessary? Are you aware that she's a very sick woman?"

"It's absolutely necessary. And I realise what this might mean for Judith Harford and Kleber if we don't stop it. Now then, how is your end working out?"

"It's not been easy. But I think we can be ready. Do you mean to continue with that arrangement now?"

"We don't have any choice. When and where do I meet you?"

"Eleven o'clock. I suggest by the church of San Nicolò on the Lido. There'll be nobody about there at that time of night. Do you know it? It's out beyond the Old Jewish Cemetery. That is if this storm doesn't break."

"I don't give a damn whether the storm breaks or not. I must have those cartoons. You'd better see that they're well packed up in polythene or something."

"My dear fellow. . ." A distinctly sour tone in his voice. "You can trust me in a matter as elementary as that at least."

"I suppose so. I'm sorry. So I'll be waiting. And you'd better bring two or three of your men with you. We might need them. I'd like to have a word with Angela Caterina now." Why hadn't I thought of it before, I wondered. It was so obvious; though I was still convinced that the little fool had never known even a quarter of what her boyfriends were really planning. But d'Espinal hesitated, and I asked sharply, "Is she there?"

"I fear not." A note just as apologetic then. "She appears to have left San Giorgio this morning; while I was out at Burano. There was nobody to stop her." He turned fretful suddenly. "We really don't seem to be doing very well."

"We're heading for a damned mess. Does she know what we're going to do tonight? And did she know that Judith and Kleber were going to be at San Francesco today?"

"As to the first, one can't be sure. For the second, I'm afraid she did. Aunt Teestock tells me she heard her making the arrangements with the Father Guardian on the telephone yesterday." He paused. "Hedley, I hope to God we're doing the right thing."

"I hope we are; for everybody's sake," I said sourly. My own temper was starting to get frayed.

Six-thirty, and another half-hour used up. I walked across restlessly to the Ca' Silvestro and then back to Harry's Bar. Nothing to see at one, except the carabinieri still on duty and a rather curious water-gate at the back of the house; nobody showing any interest in me at the other. Seven-thirty and I was at Florian's watching the crowds, half listening to the orchestra playing operatic selections, and thinking about that water-gate and the telephone call this morning.

The gate was a heavy iron grille in two wings, set in a low arch on a siding of the canal which passed right under the house; presumably where they kept their boat or boats. It was not an uncommon feature about some of the older buildings in the city; but what seemed curious was that with every other entrance closed one of the wings here was open. There could be half a dozen reasonable explanations, and there must be another locked door inside; but at the same time, if one wanted to plant an explosive where it would have the maximum effect, that was the best possible place.

And the telephone call had the same oddity about it, for if it had not come from Judith, who else could have known that we were meeting for lunch? I had certainly not told anybody, and I doubted whether she had. Kleber knew, of course, and they might have mentioned it to Father Bonnard, but I could not imagine any of them talking about it to other people; if only because so far they had all kept up an almost obsessive secrecy about everything. It was another pointer back to the Ca' Silvestro. Either there had been no message at all, or someone had taken a message and simply changed one word; and that someone therefore must have known that Judith and Hans Kleber were going to be picked up. Carson or Celia van Druyten, I wondered. So whatever happened now I had to meet Carson before I went back to the Lido.

Eight o'clock, and still no sign of any approach; the same crowd still drifting, the orchestra plunging into the Skaters' Waltz, the light turning from brassy to copperish. Eight-fifteen, and I was starting to wonder who was bluffing who; eight-thirty, and I left. Either they had taken the bait wholesale or they were now playing very carefully themselves. I was not sure which idea I liked least.

That water-gate worried me. I had a growing feeling that we were due for another surprise, and before going on to find Carson at his bar I went back to the Ca' Silvestro. It was getting dark quickly, and purely on an impulse I stopped at an electrical shop on the way and got myself a little hand torch. I did not really know why. I certainly had no conscious intention of actually trying to get into the house then. It just seemed to be something useful to have in that quiet little backwater after the glittering brilliance of the Grand Canal and the Rialto.

The place appeared to be deserted when I got there. A few lighted windows high up in some of the surrounding blocks, a closed-up building already converted into offices, a quick flash of green from the eyes of a cat prowling by the water, and the Silvestro just a black mass surrounded by its scaffolding; keeping its own secrets. There were never very many people about here even during the daytime, and now even the carabinieri seemed to have been called off. So it looked as if somebody had decided that the whole thing was a hoax after all; but I was certain now that there was something wrong, for the water-gate was still open.

There was no way of reaching it except by wading through fifteen feet or more of canal, and I went on to the next bridge and crossed that to get round to the back of the house. One of the typical little unknown squares here, nothing about it to attract anybody at night, a rather dim wall-lamp, dark archways and a few more lighted windows high up; the wall enclosing the small Ca' Silvestro backyard, another gate in decorative wrought iron. And that too was open a few inches.

A church bell somewhere close by boomed out nine strokes. Time to go and meet Carson, I told myself firmly, looking up at the black bulk of the building, hearing a burst of television music from one of the windows across the square. Nevertheless I edged in through the gate and flashed my torch across the courtyard. It picked up two more tiny green lights glaring at me for a second; a cat again, and this time slinking out of a doorway. And not even a cat can get through a locked door. I was committed then. I had to go in whether I liked it or not.

I found myself in a flagged corridor; ancient brickwork, two further arched doors on either side, a flight of stone steps going up into darkness, and a smell of petrol in the air. One door to a porter's lodge; two more to little bare cells, one stacked with builders' tools and the other with new electrical equipment and coils of wire. But the last opened into what looked like a garage workshop; a bench and tools, drums of oil, and marine tackle; and on the far side an open archway and a glint of water.

That had to be the dock under the house, the other side of the water-gate, and my light picked up a boat lying there. A big job, built on the lines of the lagoon taxies, but heavier, with a high wind and spray shield and an enclosed cabin aft; quite capable of a sixty-mile run, and certainly not the Ca' Silvestro boat. There was a faint whiff of exhaust in the air as if it had been used recently, but no sign of life about it, and I stepped down to the cockpit and ducked into the cabin. Again I had the feeling that somebody had been in here not long before, but there did not seem to be anything to see, and I was on the point of getting out when I caught a glint of something white on the carpet; a small, tightly folded wedge of paper. It looked as if it had been deliberately trodden into the angle between the floor and the side.

At that moment there was a whisper of sound from somewhere. It was impossible to localise, but it seemed to come from within the house, and I switched off the light and froze, crouching there in pitch blackness and listening for a long minute before I decided that it was only two people walking along the opposite bank of the canal outside, their voices echoing over the water. Then I flicked on the light again, snatched up the paper and got back to the landing-step to open it out. And Judith was a brilliant girl, I thought. She had taken the only means open to her of leaving proof that she and Kleber had been in that boat some time today. It was an envelope bearing a German stamp, postmarked from Munich, and addressed to Doctor Judith Harford.

My one desire now was to get out as quickly as possible. There was an atmosphere about the place which made my back hair creep; I had already found more than I had any right to expect, and by now my luck could be stretching too far. But once back in the corridor it struck me quite clearly that I could not go yet. The boat must have been brought here only after the household had left; and if Judith and Kleber had been in it during the day they might well be somewhere in the house now. It was the sort of thing these people would do; improvised, impudent, yet clever in its way because this was the last place anybody would ever expect them to be.

Whether I liked the idea or not I had to go through the place myself. It would take too long to get help from outside, and there was no telling what might happen while I was away. The first thing was light; light the whole damned place up like a gin palace, and if that brought the police in, so much the better. Looking for the switches, I made for the steps; and then I noticed a wire running down them, across the flagstones and through the workshop doorway. A clean, fine flex, lying quite loosely, as if somebody had only recently rolled it out off the reel.

The steps were built into the wall with an iron rail at one side, and it ran straight up to a square stone landing and on under another heavy door. But at least I had also found the switches; a block of four, and I slammed them all down at once. With no result. Apparently the power had been cut at the main board. There was still only the little circle of light from my own torch and the blackness above and below. And at the same time a further indefinable echo from somewhere. It seemed to be all round; a faint, hollow knocking, But impossible to tell whether it came from beneath my feet or from beyond the door, within the house itself. I stood there for a few seconds. The last thing I wanted to do was to open that door, but then I said, "To hell with this."

It had a press-down spring handle, and it seemed as if something was holding it from the other side. Then it gave suddenly. The door swung back on me with a weight behind it; and the first thing I saw was the long yellow hair. She sagged forward on to me slowly, seeming to clutch horribly at my knees as she collapsed. It was Angela Caterina; and she was not pretty any longer. She was very dead.

TEN

There was nothing anybody could do for her. It needed only a few shocked seconds to see that. She had been shot neatly in the back of the head with a small-calibre pistol, and for one sick moment I had the feeling that she herself had been knocking; trying vainly to escape. But that was impossible. She had been dead for some time; within the last few hours so far as I was competent to judge. I could only leave her lying there, and turning the circle of light away, fighting down waves of nausea, I edged past and out into another short bare passage. There was nothing here but one more door, half open; as if she had been trying to get out of the house when somebody had caught up with her.

That settled it, I thought. I had to call the *Questura*, and I went along through the next door into what appeared to be a service corridor when I flashed the light along it. A dull brown carpet, a serving-trolley standing against one wall, a faint odour of cooking, innocent and domestic; yet more doors, one in studded red leather, and the wire running on to disappear under another at the far end. An aroma of cigar smoke and liquor beyond that one. Carson's living quarters, for the torch wavered over crowded furniture, bottles and decanters on a sideboard, a roll top desk and a telephone there. That was the only possible answer now. The wire running into this room, and what was lying out at the head of the steps ought to be more than enough to interest even Alberti.

Then just as I was about to lift the receiver there was another sound, clear and distinct this time, from the corridor outside. I found myself picked up in a sudden glare of light. It came from the doorway, and as I swung round a voice said, "Let that alone!"

We stood for a few seconds, my feeble little torch picking up Carson, his nearly blinding me. Then he went on, "It's you, is it. I was expecting you at Benito's."

"So you were," I agreed. "So why did you come back?"

"Nosing, are you?" he asked. "I live here, don't I? Just things I have to see to. I reckon we'd better have a bit of light on the scene."

"It would be a relief," I said.

"Don't go running away, will you? I'll only be just along the passage. I want to know what the hell you're doing." He paused. "And for Christ's sake leave that telephone alone."

"I won't run away," I promised.

He disappeared, and I took a quick look; and the thought of what might have happened if I had lifted the receiver made my blood run cold. The telephone itself was the switch. Devised to activate on somebody calling the house from outside; and Carson appeared to think it might operate just as well if anybody called out from here, but he had no means of knowing that I had already traced the wire and guessed what it was for He had given himself away. I could use that telephone to frighten the wits out of him; and frightened men talk fast.

I was leaning innocently against the desk when he came back and flicked on the overhead lights. He seemed friendly enough, and he asked, "What about a drink to start with?"

"That would be another relief." I watched him pouring two generous measures of Scotch and decided to force the pace, to learn as much as possible and then get out. "You do yourself pretty well, don't you?" I asked. "Aren't you going to miss all this if anything happens tonight?"

"Everything's got to end some time. The old woman's sick, you know. She's dying of cancer. The quacks give her six months." He shrugged and took a long swallow of his drink. "You've got to be sorry for her; but you've got to look after yourself as well, and this place ain't much use to anybody. She's left it to the City of Venice. With her portrait; what you're painting. It's an honour for you, ain't it?"

"It is." And I meant that. "So then you're out. But if I know the old lady I'll bet she's left you something too."

"It won't go far these days. Look here, cock," he blustered suddenly, "it's you supposed to be talking, not me. I still want to know what you're doing here."

"I happened to be walking past and saw the water-gate was open, so I thought I'd better take a look inside. Do you know there's a boat down there? All ready for a long trip?" His face did not give anything away, and I went on, "I found something else too. I think the police ought to see it, and I'm calling them now."

"No!" It was almost a scream. "For God's sake leave

that thing alone."

"Why? What's wrong with it?"

"Nothing. There's nothing wrong." He was sweating visibly. "We just don't want that lot around, that's all. The old woman's been up to some funny little games of her own. You don't know the Eytie coppers like we do. Look," he asked desperately, "why don't we go along to Benito's?"

"What for? We've already got drinks here. Better than we shall get anywhere else, and they're on the house." With one hand still on the telephone I held out my glass to him in the other, at arm's length. If I had not been so frightened myself I should have enjoyed playing with him. As he poured the drink his own hand shook so much that I heard the bottle clinking. I said, "If anybody talks it has to be you."

He tried bluster again. "What the hell are you up to? And who's this Contessa di Lampedusa? I never heard of her before."

"There's a lot you haven't heard of. And you must be a fool if you trust Donato. Once they've got those cartoons across to Porec you'll whistle for your cut. Even if they don't fix it for you to carry the can for the whole thing."

That startled him afresh. "How do you know about Porec?"

"I know it all." I looked at my watch, surprised myself to find that it was still only just half-past nine. Providing I could break Carson down quickly enough I could still get across to the Lido by eleven. I went on, "We'd better hurry up. D'Espinal's going to call me here at a quarter to ten."

"He's what?" His voice rose to another scream. "For Christ's sake, I'm getting out of this."

"If you do I'll call the polic before you get to the door. What's worrying you, anyhow? I'm offering you a deal. So let's get on with it. When the old lady agreed to evacuate today you called the others and told them the house was all theirs. Is that right.

He nodded. "They reckoned the way things was shaping they'd best move tonight." He broke off, staring at me. "And you put the old woman up to that."

"So what time did they come here?"

"About seven. Just after we was all out. I left 'em to it."

"What was Angela Caterina doing with them?"

He grinned faintly. "Making a bloody nuisance of herself, like usual. She wanted them to take her when they left, and threatening to split on 'em if they didn't."

"They came in the boat?" He nodded. "And they brought two other people."

"Listen," he started, "I didn't have anything to do with that."

"Who's going to believe you? You're in trouble, Carson. Conspiracy, murder and kidnapping. The others will get away with it because they've got family pull and the money, and you'll carry the can. But if you like to think if over for a minute or two I'm in no hurry. Why don't you have another drink before d'Espinal calls? It'll very likely be your last. Unless you care to tell me now. Where are Miss Harford and Dr Kleber?"

"Too true it'll be my last," he screamed. "And yours. The first ring of that bell and the lot goes sky-high." His face was pasty and mottled; flecks of spittle at the corners of his mouth. "God damn you," he whispered, "they're down below; in the cellars. There's a door under the steps. You'd never see it unless. . ."

"Unless you showed me? So why don't you?"

I was sweating myself, and I could smell the sweat and fear floating back from Carson as he lumbered ahead of me. It is a curious fact that if he had tried anything then I should have knocked him cold without a second thought, yet I have always regretted what followed. I had pushed him too far and he was over-weight with years of soft living; when we reached the landing at the top of the steps, with Angela Caterina lying there, he stopped dead. His breath was already coming in rattling gasps, and he choked at the sight of her in the harsh light of a naked, overhead bulb.

"Christ Almighty," he breathed. "Oh, my God. Did you do that?"

I said, "Don't be a fool. Did you?"

His voice rose. "What d'you take me for? That bastard Donato . . . Oh my God, I wish I'd never got mixed up. . ."

He choked again, tried to reach for the handrail but clutched at his chest instead, doubled forward with a grunt of pain, and then rolled helplessly down the steps before I could stop him. He bumped down all eighteen of them, steep, sharp-edged stone, gaining momentum with each one, and reached the bottom before I started down myself. It was too late then. Even if the heart attack had not killed him before he actually started to fall, his head was lying at an ugly unnatural angle. It was only a matter of form to feel for his pulse; and at the same time there was a dull, muffled hammering coming from somewhere close by.

I said foolishly, "I'm sorry about that, Carson," and then left him to go and find the door. Even with the lights on it was difficult. A deep archway under the steps, almost invisible ancient timber, and when I dragged that open another passage beyond. The damned place was all doors and passages, I thought furiously, but the hammering was clearer and louder now, coming from another at the end. That was the last, creaking horribly as I unlocked and pulled it back, Kleber's voice demanding, "Who is that?" myself answering, "Hedley," and then a second later Judith clinging to me. I said, "Now let's get out, fast. There's an explosive charge down here somewhere and it only wants one telephone call. . ."

I imagined it was all over then, starting to breathe again; but I did not yet know Herr Kleber. After so long in the dark they were dazzled by the light, and I got them out to the courtyard, hurrying past Carson; but then Kleber asked, "What was that you said, Mr Hedley? Something about an explosive charge, and the telephone?"

Considering that he was by no means a young man and must have had a very uncomfortable day he was remarkably self-possessed; tired and showing signs of strain, yet he seemed to be rather cooler than I was myself at that moment. I explained quickly, and he nodded. "Yes; I see," and then went on, "Judith, I think you should leave; but I shall be grateful for your assistance, Mr Hedley."

"What are you going to do?" I asked, but he was turning back into the house. I muttered, "For God's sake . . ." and started after him, but then realised that Judith was following me too and hissed at her, "You get out of it at least." She answered simply, "I'm terrified, but nuts." And I said, "We're all nuts." I called, "Herr Kleber, this is crazy. It needs an expert."

"Mr Hedley," he announced calmly, "I *am* an expert; or I was, many years ago." He was already tracing the wire across the workshop and he came back to run his eye over the bench, take a tool here and there, and nod approvingly at a portable inspection-lamp on a long flex. "Everything we need," he murmured, completely in command. "Amelita Messina-Silvestro would never forgive me if I failed to disarm that thing."

"If it goes off there'll be nothing left of any of us to

forgive," I told him brutally.

"True," he admitted. "You have a point there. Now if you will be good enough to bring the lamp for me."

There was nothing else I could do. The man even seemed to be enjoying himself in a quiet way, and he found the bomb in a few seconds. It was in a deep recess about chest high in the wall, a package wrapped in polythene. He appeared to be pleased with it. "A small charge," he said. " 'Not so deep as a well, nor so wide as a church door: but 'tis enough.' " I heard him snipping at something, and he went on, "It appears to be fairly unsophisticated; but it might be unwise simply to cut the wire. As you probably know, Mr Hedley, an explosive substance is merely an unstable compound which tends to return violently to stability."

"That's an enchanting thought," I said feelingly.

"I wish I had your sense of humour." There was more snipping. "As I said, many years ago I was an expert; in the army here in Italy. That is how I came to meet the Messina-Silvestro family." At that point he caught his breath sharply, and I flinched. He asked mildly, "Can you hold the lamp higher? Over my shoulder." And went on quietly again, "And as I was considered to be useless for anything more heroic I was placed in charge of a demolition company. I learned quite a lot about explosives."

Glancing back at Judith watching us silently from the archway, I thought that one could only hope he had learned enough.

"It's an extraordinary thing that what seemed to be so much useless experience then should now prove to be so valuable." I was beginning to suspect that Herr Kleber had his own curious sense of humour, but he seemed to be getting to the ticklish part of the operation then, for he stopped talking. Another suspended two minutes; and then he breathed, 'I think that's drawn its teeth," and held up a little copper cylinder hanging from the wire. There was a distinct glint of amusement in his eye. He said, "One likes to make a small contribution."

I heard Judith take a deep breath, and saw her close her eyes, but Herr Kleber had not finished yet. He looked at the boat thoughtfully. "Those young men today annoyed me intensely. I should hate to see them escape. I feel sure you could do something there with these pliers, Mr Hedley."

I could and did. I got a savage pleasure out of it. Five minutes' concentrated work, and by the time I had finished nothing would start that motor. Then I said, "Now for God's sake let's get out of here."

It came almost as a shock to see the lights and crowds on the Grand Canal, but we did not linger there. It was then ten-fifteen, and I was determined to see the job out now. I told them briefly what I had planned with d'Espinal and Emilia Pentecost—which seemed to amuse Kleber again—then I called the *Questura* from a bar, said simply that there had been two people killed at the Ca' Silvestro and hung up before they had time to ask who I was. After that we mingled with the crowds, walked back to San Marco and took a taxi for the Lido; when Judith and Kleber went on with their side of the story.

It had been ridiculously simple. Judith had called the Ca' Silvestro that morning in fact to confirm that they were meeting me, and Carson had merely changed a few words of the message. When they left the monastery there had been what appeared to be a taxi at the landing-stage, or at least the two men driving it had been wearing taxi-caps and badges. They had got into it quite unsuspectingly, and only when it was too late had they realised that instead of heading back towards Venice it was racing up into the northern lagoon. They had been put ashore on a small completely deserted island on which the only building was what Kleber described as an old fisherman's night shelter; and here they had found Piretti and the bearded man called George waiting for them. These two had been perfectly polite, had even got a meal of sorts for them, but had kept them in the building all the afternoon until about six o'clock when Donato appeared. And Donato had a gun.

"One does not argue with that type," Kleber said. "They have what you would call a kink in their minds. I have met them before." He smiled at me. "Again, many years ago."

They had all come back to the Ca' Silvestro in the boat I had put out of action; and Donato had told Kleber and Judith that if they were prepared to co-operate they would come to no harm in the end. If they were not . . . Kleber shrugged. "He made his meaning sufficiently clear. I thought it was advisable to appear to be much more docile than either of us really felt." He glanced at me quizzically. "And Judith was sublimely confident that you would find us."

She flushed brilliantly. "Well, he did, didn't he?"

I felt it was best not to tell her that I had sat around for several hours doing nothing; and there was an almost continuous flicker of lightning far off and low down in the sky.

Eleven twenty-five, and I was standing in full view at the ferry station. The Viale Elizabetta was still blazing with lights, but with the approaching storm there were very few people about; the big ferry was lying motionless, nobody going abroad and the man at the rail apparently half asleep. I had met d'Espinal at San Nicoló, he had handed me the bulky roll, and I had told him briefly about Angela Caterina. He had taken it in ominous silence, and then he and the boat, with three more men in it, had vanished into the darkness.

Two of them would get on to the ferry; d'Espinal would remain in the boat and keep pace with it across the lagoon. So far as we could we had covered every possibility. There was just a chance that somebody might have gone back to the Ca' Silvestro and walked straight into the police, who must be there in force by now. But I did not think they would do that. I thought they would stay over this side and concentrate everything on getting the cartoons.

But there was no time to speculate. A bell rang sharply, and I hurried on to the ferry and round to the stern seats, behind the midships superstructure, where Antonello must have been the other night. I sat with the big roll across my knees, and the rail-man closed the gate with a clang and disappeared up the stairs to the top deck; d'Espinal's two men, Kleber and Judith and probably some police would all be up there, but so far as I could see in the dim lighting there did not seem to be anybody else down here. Twenty minutes to get across, and if anything happened at all it would be about halfway. Out over the lagoon a long fork of lightning rippled across the sky again.

In fact it started before we got halfway, although quietly at first. A further flash of lightning picked up one figure and then another appearing from round the central block; and two more behind them. A glistening black plastic raincoat and a white face. She said, "Give me that, Mr Hedley."

The one with her was the bearded man, George, the others strangers; and toughs. But no sign of Donato or Piretti. The unexpected again, I thought, but I asked, "Miss van Druyten? What are you doing here?"

"Isn't it obvious? Give me that roll; quickly. We don't want a fuss."

George had a hand torch, flashing it over the side. So they had another boat standing by. It was quite obvious; they could cruise alongside, pick up these four people and the cartoons perfectly safely over the low rail, and then get to the Ca' Silvestro long before the ferry even touched San Zaccaria. But d'Espinal should be out there somewhere by now. I had to keep talking for a few minutes to give him time to see what was going on. I said, "So you're double-crossing the old lady as well, are you?"

That seemed to flick her on a sensitive spot. "You should mind your own business. I've had that old woman for the last ten years."

"You should mind yours," I told her deliberately. "Carson's dead. And they've murdered Angela Caterina. You've got yourself into trouble, lady."

"What d'you mean?" It startled and frightened her, but she said, "That's nonsense. Now give us those cartoons."

I glanced over the rail. Their boat was there now with Donato and Piretti, riding easily alongside and holding on. Another flash of lightning picked up d'Espinal coming in. This was the moment, and I flung the roll at her, yelling, "You can have it then!" But at the same time Judith and Kleber appeared from the stairs. I had begged them to keep well out of it, but Judith was bristling like an angry cat and Kleber obviously meant to join in. I saw van Druyten dropping the cartoons, and starting to get over after them yelled, "Stop her!" at Kleber, and jack-knifed one of the toughs. But the other two got me, and what followed then was confused. I glimpsed Kleber and Judith dragging van Druyten back, men appearing from everywhere, heard bells clanging and footsteps thundering down the stairs all in a split second as I went out and down deep into the water myself.

I came up choking and cursing. Donato's boat was now roaring away, but the ferry's engines had stopped although it was still drifting on. There seemed to be a considerable fight in progress on the lower deck, and I could just see Judith staring out over the rail, but then a headlight swung round and picked me up, and I struck out towards it. A minute later I was being dragged in, d'Espinal standing up and waving his arms like a windmill, bawling, "We have him! And now," he roared at his driver, "follow those rascals. Fast!"

I coughed out several more gallons of lagoon and said, "There's no need. They're heading for the Ca' Silvestro and they'll run straight into the police there."

And then there was a murderous crash of thunder and the heavens opened. I never heard what d'Espinal answered, but Pietro opened the throttle and we shot away like a hydroplane through streaming sheets of water. The ferry disappeared behind us, the waterfront lights brightened into a silvery blur, and almost before I had time to bawl at d'Espinal again that there was no need for this we were racing past the Molo and entering the Grand Canal. Fortunately that was nearly clear, everything driven in by the sudden deluge. But there were still police launches about. We had barely passed under the Accademia Bridge before there was a howl of the first siren and then another behind us. I said, "This is going to be one hell of a party."

It turned out to be more like a shambles. Donato and Piretti must have been just a minute or so ahead of us as we swung into the dock with the police launches close behind. We had to cut our motor to get in, but they appeared to have taken it too fast, for the nose of their boat was crumpled again the far wall. It was impossible to know whether they had surprised the police already in the house, or whether the police had surprised them. The place was blazing with lights, and Piretti was frantically trying to start the bigger boat, while Donato was crouched behind its cabin; with a pistol in his hand. The police appeared to be in the workshop beyond the arch; at such an angle that neither could get a clear shot at the others. Donato was chillingly cool. He was saying, "Listen. There's an explosive here. You let us get out; or I blow it."

Piretti screamed, "Don't!" and one of the police fired blindly from the arch. We ourselves were slewed in the gate, nudged from behind by the other launches, and Donato stared at us coldly for a second, half swivelled the gun on me, but then changed his mind. He said, "So we can't get out; so if that's the way you want it," and took deliberate aim. I saw brick-dust fly from the side of the recess, and Piretti screamed again. Donato took fresh aim, still more carefully, resting his elbows on the cabin-top to steady himself; and this time I knew he was going to get it.

I thought we ought to have taken the thing out and dropped it in the water. My own voice surprised me. I croaked, "It's not there, Donato. It's been taken out."

He laughed at me. "Don't fool yourself. I can see it. And I'll blow it, if only for the sake of getting you."

Then our boat rocked violently as police from the launch behind scrambled over into it, and he shifted and took a snap shot at us. I heard it whine past my ear. One of the policemen grunted and cursed, and Donato fired twice more in quick succession at the explosive. Dust flew out of the recess itself, and there was a flash of lightning outside, a crash of thunder which for a second I thought actually was the explosion; but at the same time somebody behind us fired back. Three shots one after the other; and Donato jerked and twisted and slid down quietly behind the cabin.

The place seemed to be full of police suddenly, coming from everywhere, and I was sick and tired of the whole business. I thought that now it was going to be a long and unpleasant night.

It was extremely unpleasant, but the real enquiry came

next morning in the *Questura*, in the captain's office; the man who had been at Mrs Messina-Silvestro's cocktail party. The cartoons were lying on his desk; with the exception of Celia van Druyten we were all there, even Emilia Pentecost and the Professor Venturi from the Accademia; and the captain was hot, angry and harassed. With Alberti watching me expressionlessly I had told my story from the balloon man to the events last night, and when I finished the captain breathed, "Dear Jesus; the Donatos and the Pirettis. How we shall quieten this I do not know. I have a thought that we should do well to ask you to leave Venice, Signor Hedley."

"Mr Hedley will remain in Venice as long as he wishes," Mrs Messina-Silvestro said crisply. "As my guest."

He glowered at me balefully. "There is still much I do not understand. This camerman." He riffled among the papers on the desk. "George Marshall. Another Englishman. Why to begin with did he take those films?"

"They kept changing their plans," I explained again patiently. "They were getting information from Miss van Druyten and the girl Angela Caterina, but they did not realise at first that Miss Harford and Dr Kleber actually know each other very well. Their first idea was to pick up Miss Harford, arrange for another young woman to impersonate her and lure Dr Kleber to some place where he also could have been kidnapped without any trouble. When they saw they couldn't succeed they started to think of something else."

He closed his eyes. "But why should they *want* to kidnap the Doctors Kleber and Harford?"

"To authenticate the cartoons; and as hostages. If they had got away with those Mrs Messina-Silvestro would have repudiated them, of course. She would have said she had never even heard of them. Without certificates by two absolutely unimpeachable authorities they would have been almost unsaleable." I was getting irritated.

"Ah yes, the cartoons." The captain smirked slightly. "We will come to the cartoons in their order." He turned the glower on Alberti. "So who is this Marshall? Is he connected with the other film comapny? Those we have been instructed to assist?"

"He is merely a hanger-on in Venice; with Antonio Donato. Donato was of that sort. He had no connection with the correct film company. They have never heard of him. He was to remain here after the others had left and make the telephone call to fire the explosive. The woman van Druyten refused to do that."

Alberti glanced at Mrs Messina-Silvestro, but she did not say anything, and the captain came back to me. "And now, Signor Hedley, what in God's name was the need for the charade on the ferry last night?"

"Was it a charade? I didn't think so. It's quite simple. Nobody wanted to believe that Donato and Jo Piretti were involved. That seemed the easiest way of proving it." It was my turn to ask Alberti something. "Who were those other men on the ferry?"

"Two types from the Via Garibaldi," Alberti said. "The sort who will do anything for a sufficient fee; nobodies."

"Thank God somebody is nobodies," the captain exploded. "The Donatos. And the Pirettis. Dear God, with people like these governments have fallen for less."

"No doubt," Mrs Messina-Silvestro agreed evenly. "And police chiefs. But with the governments we suffer these days it does not make much difference."

That produced a frozen silence for a few seconds, but then the captain prepared to get his own back. He tapped the cartoons with his finger, ominously. "Now we come to these. To me they are indecent, but no matter. It is our great Leonardo. And I am informed, signora, that you are planning to sell them abroad; for an immense sum of money. The property of the Italian state and people. Is that correct?"

"Why not?" she asked coolly. "Will you be good enough to tell the captain what those things are worth, Sir Harcourt."

D'Espinal shrugged magnificently. "A few hundred perhaps; pounds or dollars. As curiosities. If one can find a buyer. They are forgeries."

"A few hundred?" the captain repeated incredulously. The baleful glare turned back on Alberti. "I understood . . . millions."

"Such ridiculous rumours," Mrs Messina-Silvestro snapped. "I cannot imagine how they got about. That foolish companion of mine, I suppose. But perhaps Professor Venturi here will decide for us. I imagine you will take the word of a director of the Accademia, captain?"

Professor Venturi still looked like an ancient parrot, as he had at Mrs Messina-Silvestro's party. He pecked and bowed at the cartoons, making a big thing of it, examining them from all angles, almost rubbing his beak in them, but it was obvious that he had spotted it in the first few seconds. "Forgeries," he announced at last. I half expected him to ask, "Who's a clever bird then?" He nodded and pecked happily. "Good in their way; even excellent. But I should hesitate to believe that Leonardo would descend to such work. I would say early to the middle eighteenth century. Would you not agree, Sir Harcourt?"

D'Espinal inclined his head graciously. "My dear professor, I bow to your superior expertise. I would not dare to disagree."

Emilia said nothing. She was smiling faintly. Clever, clever Emilia Pentecost, I thought. She must have worked like the devil yesterday to produce those drawings, and they were extraordinarily good; even slightly smudged and aged and on the right sort of paper.

"Forgeries," Dr Hans Kleber said. He was enjoying himself again. I was getting to like that man's sense of humour more and more every minute.

"Quite, quite certainly forgeries," said Dr Judith Harford of Boston.

Mrs Messina-Silvestro pushed herself up stiffly but regally, gathering us all around her like a retinue. "So I imagine there is no more to say, Captain Sabbioni."

The last scene was where it ought to be; in the roof-top restaurant of the Danieli with a pretty girl on another beautiful blue translucent evening. The food was uninspired, but the view was superb. Judith was wearing the purple and gold caftan, though without any of the other trimmings of the Contessa di Lampedusa. She was slightly severe at first.

"We ought not to rejoice," she announced. "That silly girl. And Celia van Druyten. And Mrs Messina-Silvestro herself. Is that true about her?"

I said, "I'm afraid it is. But it doesn't seem to worry her. She says she's done all she wants to do. And she refuses to bring any charges against van Druyten. She's managed to convince the police that neither Celia nor Carson had anything to do with the murders. In fact she probably told them; and I fancy the police don't want to make too much fuss in view of the other people involved. And she told van Druyten to go away and take a holiday."

There was silence for a time, and then Judith asked, "What about the cartoons? The real ones?"

"D'Espinal will simply take them out under his arm on a flight to Munich. Nobody will be the slightest bit interested."

She regarded me thoughtfully. "Is that why they got you to do the portrait? Because you have those sort of ideas?"

"I began to suspect they were using me. But it really was Mrs Messina who wanted the portrait. D'Espinal and Emilia Pentecost simply thought I was the best man for the job. And they felt they could trust me if I did notice anything."

"I like a little becoming modesty." There was another silence before she went on, "She said something about you staying in Venice as her guest. Are you really going to stay at the Ca' Silvestro?"

"God forbid," I said feelingly. "The Martinelli suits me well enough."

She murmured, "Yes. That suits me very well too."